ARCHENEMY

BOOK 1 OF THE XAVIER TRILOGY

CHRISTINA BAUER

COPYRIGHT

Newton, MA 02464
www.monsterhousebooks.com
ISBN 9781956114522

First Edition

DEDICATION

For All Those Who Kick Ass, Take Names and Read Books

CONTENTS

ARCHENEMY

ALSO BY CHRISTINA BAUER

APPENDIX

BONUS IMAGES

COLLECTED WORKS

CHRISTINA BAUER, AUTHOR

Angelbound Xavier

The real story behind our favorite archangel

1. Archenemy
2. Archnemesis
3. Archangel

Angelbound Origins

About a quasi (part demon and part human) girl who loves kicking butt in Purgatory's Arena

1. Angelbound
2. Scala
3. Acca
4. Thrax
5. The Dark Lands
6. The Brutal Time
7. Armageddon
8. Quasi Redux
9. Clockwork Igni
10. Lady Reaper
11. Reaper Games

12. Angry Gods
13. Phantom Corsair

Angelbound Offspring

The next generation takes on Heaven, Hell, and everything in between

1. Maxon
2. Portia
3. Zinnia
4. Rhodes
5. Kaps
6. Mack
7. Huntress
8. Gage

**This is a finished series.*

Angelbound Lincoln

The Angelbound experience as told by Prince Lincoln

1. Duty Bound
2. Lincoln
3. Trickster
4. Baculum
5. Angelfire
6. Rixa
7. Mordred

Fairy Tales of the Magicorum

Modern fairy tales with sass, action, and romance

1. Wolves and Roses
2. Moonlight and Midtown
3. Shifters and Glyphs
4. Slippers and Thieves
5. Bandits and Ball Gowns
6. Fire and Cinder
7. Fairies and Frosting
8. Towers and Tithes

9. Evil Queens and Goblin Kings

Dimension Drift

Dystopian adventures with science, snark, and hot aliens

1. Scythe
2. Umbra
3. Alien Minds
4. ECHO Academy
5. Justice
6. Slate

Pixieland Diaries

1. Pixieland Diaries
2. Calla
3. Dare
4. Winter Prince
5. Ley Queen

**This is a finished series.*

Beholder

Where a medieval farm girl discovers necromancy and true love

1. Cursed
2. Concealed
3. Cherished
4. Crowned
5. Cradled

**This is a completed series.*

ARCHENEMY

Mortimer

1

XAVIER

ENGLAND, 2770 BCE

The first rays of dawn touch the forest outside my hut. Gentle breezes shake the oaks, setting off a chorus of rustling leaves. The scent of all things green and fresh fills the air. Inside my home, mice skitter around the straw pile that serves as my bed. Months ago, those little creatures might have snapped me out of a deep sleep.

But I'm already awake. Why? I've avoided any slumber for the last six weeks. It's not easy, yet I have no choice.

Because when I dream, I see *her*.

The woman in red.

Lying on my back, I lace my fingers behind my head and wonder who's behind these unwanted night visions. All the while, I *don't* think about the woman in red. I don't picture her ruby-colored hair and matching dress. Or how her wide eyes gleam with intelligence while her full mouth appears ripe for a kiss. And I definitely ignore the way she exudes feline grace with every movement. The very core of my being craves her. Again.

And I'm not even dreaming. This is bad.

I'm a warrior angel. Since the dawn of time, I've only focused on battle. Women are to be protected, not desired. And especially not a quasi-demonic lady who sports a dragon scale tail… like the one in my dream.

Crunch! Crunch!

Uneven footsteps sound on the dried-out leaves outside my hut. I know that particular stride. It's Mortimer, High Druid of Stonehenge. Normally, I dread the fellow coming around. Now, I welcome any distraction.

The footsteps stop. Mortimer starts chanting something about the coming of summer and visiting the great god, Cernunnos. This kind of thing can go on for hours if I don't break it up early.

"Come in!" I call.

Mortimer stops chanting. He slides away the panel of thatched branches that serves as my door.

Mortimer's a lanky fellow in loose black robes. His long face holds a pinched nose and a full beard. Like always, he carries a staff topped by a round stone. After stepping inside my hut, he bows in my direction.

"I greet thee, Oh God of the Wild, Cernunnos."

When I first moved here from the desert realm, I tried explaining how I'm an angel from Heaven. It didn't go well. Humans don't handle strange things easily. Eventually, the druids decided that I am actually Cernunnos, their forest god. One day, humans may know angels so well, I'll be forced to hide my identity. For now, I consider the 'Cernunnos mistake' to be a step in the right direction.

I sit up on my straw bed. "And greetings to you, Mortimer the Druid."

"You live in filth." Sadly, Mortimer knows I'm not the smiting sort of deity. He sasses off all the time.

"You're not wrong." My hut is filled with spell ingredients. Herbs hang in bunches from the ceiling. Other magical supplies—everything from new seeds to old dragon scales—lie in wooden bowls on the floor. Packets of pre-made spells sit everywhere. "I should clean up."

"It's not your dwelling I refer to, but you, oh Cernunnos."

"You're not wrong there, either."

Dust covers my dark skin. My hair is matted, as is my uneven beard. What were once pristine robes are now rags. And my white wings are speckled with dirt.

I'm a total mess. And it's all because of her.

"Ah, that." I purse my lips and debate what I should tell Mortimer. The short answer is, *not much*. Sadly, my sleepy mind has other ideas.

"I'm having dreams again," I admit. "Fantastical stuff."

"Oh!" Mortimer rubs his palms together. "In these night visions, do you live in a golden palace and consult with the king and queen of the desert realm?"

Mortimer is talking about my friend, the god Osiris, and his wife, the goddess Isis. I lived with them for years before Osiris died. It's not something I discuss. Ever.

"I told you about that?"

"Yes, at the half moon."

"Guess I'm sleepier than I thought." I rub my eyes. "My adventures in the desert realm are not a fantasy. That was my life before I came here."

"Ah." Mortimer runs his bony fingers through his long brown beard. "Perhaps you've been dreaming how the god Osiris taught you the secrets of spell casting?"

I lift my brows in surprise. "I told you about that, too?"

"At the quarter moon."

"I'm *far* sleepier than I thought." I bob my head, trying to find the words to explain everything to Mortimer. "Although my time with Osiris may sound like a fantasy, it actually happened. And Osiris is the God of Reincarnation."

Mortimer wags his finger at me. "Do not say such things. You are Cernunnos. Other deities do not exist. Your blasphemy will bring down wrath on our people."

I debate about correcting Mortimer, but he's more skittish than most druids. "Perhaps we've visited enough for one day."

"Come now, tell me what troubles your dreams." Mortimer sits down beside me on the pile of straw. "Start with these *fantasies* about Osiris. Perhaps that will help."

Memories appear. *It's two hundred years ago. I wear my desert realm garb of a linen kilt and slippers. My head is shaved and my skin is slick with sweat. Heat beats down on me as I race along the Nile, calling for Osiris. Panic zings through my limbs. Questions ricochet through my mind.*

Where is Osiris?

How could I allow him to confront his unpredictable brother, Set, alone?

I speed along for what feels like hours, calling for my friend the entire time. Some humans offer to aid in the search. I gently refuse their help. No humans can see Osiris, let alone track him. At last, I discover a body lying in the reeds by the Nile. Rough wounds cover his torso—the kind of slices that can only be made by Set's massive sword.

It's Osiris. He's dead.

For a long moment, it's all I can do to stare at the corpse. Osiris is gone.

"Xavier, did you hear me?"

I blink hard, pushing the recollection away. "Yes, Mortimer?"

"You were about to share the tale of Osiris." Mortimer sets his hand on my shoulder. "I came here to check on you. Allow me to do that. Talk to me."

Guilt weighs on my shoulders. I should never have let Osiris face Set alone. Now, my adopted brother rules the Duat underworld where he exists as an undead thing. I'll never see him again. It's why I came to the Northlands in the first place—I must forget Osiris. Perhaps moving here was a mistake. I thought life in a different culture would help me. Instead, I dream about a woman in red.

Life here isn't working. *Time to move on.*

Rising, I begin collecting all my spell packets into a single leather satchel. "Actually, it's beyond time for me to leave. I've always wanted to live somewhere with more snow than rain. I'm sure you understand."

"You're going now?" Mortimer stands as well. "That isn't a good idea."

Snap!

Suddenly, the packed earth cracks around Mortimer's feet. Lines of red mist rise up from the ground. The tendrils of smoke twist into the shape of ghostly faces. All of them are screaming. None make a sound.

A chill runs down my back. Mortimer's eyes take on a frantic expression. His mouth stretches into an unnaturally large smile. The tendrils of red smoke keep twisting around his body.

This isn't Mortimer anymore. Someone else has possessed my friend.

"Who are you and what have you done with Mortimer?"

It's Mortimer who speaks, but another, deeper voice comes from his mouth. "Your druid friend is in this body, but he is no longer the ruler of his own flesh. You now speak with the maker of your dreams. I'm the one who created the woman in red."

Only one entity tells you he's magically invading your night visions. My skin prickles over in shock.

"I know who you are. Set, the God of Chaos."

"Correct."

The word hits me with such force, I have trouble pulling air into my lungs. After all, I came to the Northlands to escape memories of Osiris' death. Now, the deity responsible for killing my friend is tormenting me with dreams of the perfect woman.

More red smoke rises and twists around Mortimer's body. When the haze clears, the druid is gone. Instead, an eight-foot-tall humanoid looms before me. The man has dark skin that glistens as if he were just dipped in blood. He wears the garb of a pharaoh. And there's no missing his donkey ears and aardvark snout.

That's Set, all right.

Set

2

XAVIER

Set looms before me. Chaos magic radiates from him with such force, I feel the energy rattling my bones.

"Where's the gratitude?" asks Set. "I send you dreams of the perfect woman, and you've not a single word of thanks. It took me ages to design a woman to trap you… Perhaps even cut your throat while you sleep. I even took inspiration from other realities, just to ensure you'd be powerless to refuse her."

"Other realities?"

"You can't think this is the only version of us in existence. And chaos knows no boundaries."

A familiar mix of anger and frustration twists up my back. I open my mouth, ready to counter that I'll never fall for Set's 'chaos woman.'

I stop myself before speaking a word. Claiming I don't care for this dream lady doesn't ring true, even inside my own mind. The reason is simple. For years, I've lived in the woods with only Mortimer and his predecessors for companionship. A beautiful woman is a good way to grab my attention. And this is Set's classic mode of attack—chaos and distraction.

"I see what you're doing," I state. "I'm supposed to worry about the woman in red and avoid the true risk here."

"Ah, you refer to my wish to annihilate all life on Earth." Set grins. "It's what I do, isn't it? Remember when great lizards roamed the land? I wiped them out. But it was an unfinished eradication. Human life should never have been able to rise up. Now I must finish my extermination."

"This is all based on one assumption."

"And that is?"

"You've actually escaped your prison under the Red Pyramid." Now, it's my turn to smile. "I don't believe you're free."

Set chuckles. "You are clever. I see why Osiris kept you around. Too bad you weren't wise enough to stop dear my dear brother from fighting me alone. I plunged my blade into his heart."

My blood heats with rage. *How can he talk about murdering Osiris?* I force my breathing to slow. *This is simply another distraction. Don't play into his schemes.*

"As I said before, I won't be lured away from what's important here. Did you escape, yes or no?"

"Of course, I am free. Can you really believe that Osiris' silly boy, Horus, would cast a strong enough spell to keep me imprisoned forever?"

Set does have a point. Horus insisted it was his blood right to imprison Set. It was more of a drunken rampage. The move was so unexpected, it even caught the God of Chaos by surprise. No one thinks Set will stay trapped forever.

I purse my lips and consider. If Set has really escaped, I'd have a dagger in my throat, same as Osiris.

This is all a lie.

Even so, I must test my theory. Glancing around my hut, I spy the pre-made packet for a spell of revealment. All I need is enough time to cast it. Set isn't the only one who can use distractions.

"How's life under the Red Pyramid?" I ask. "You're trapped in a great cavern made entirely of onyx. What chaotic illusions you must conjure in order to pass the time."

"I picture killing you, often. Do you wish to kill me?"

"Attack me and find out."

"I spend my time thinking about a single question. Why did my brother, Osiris, save you?"

With these words, more memories flood my mind. I recall the day I met Osiris. It was the War of the Clouds. Angels and demons fought in the sky over the desert realm. I was one of the many who were wounded. I fell from the clouds to land on the desert below. Bodies and blood were everywhere. Osiris came by, picked me up from the battlefield and healed me. Afterward, he taught me spell craft for years.

"I don't know why Osiris picked me," I admit. "Just as I don't know why he insisted on fighting you alone." I meet Set's gaze. His blood-red eyes seem to shine with a potent mixture of jealousy and rage.

"That can't be true. You must know." With that, one thing is clear. At last, the God of Chaos is fully distracted.

Here's my chance.

Scooping up the spell packet, I rush to kneel at Set's feet, right at the spot where the ground first cracked open before Mortimer. Crushing the packet in my hand, I press the ingredients against the broken earth and focus on the angelic magic within me. A chill pools behind my eyes—that means my irises are glowing blue with angel power. I speak the incantation.

Truth and dawn
Lies be gone

Energy and magic surge up my arms. White light erupts from the ingredients I've pressed against the cracked soil. Pale beams shine out from between my fingers and onto Sets' long robes.

I look up. If the spell works, then the ground will seal over and Set will vanish. That isn't what happens.

"I summon my chaos." Set raises his arms. "Give me the truth!"

Ssssss!

Fresh plumes of red smoke erupt from the break in the ground.

Waves of chaos energy move through me. It's as if insects are crawling under my skin. Crimson mist soon fills my hut.

Boom!

The walls of my home blast apart, revealing the oak forest beyond. As always, no one is near, except for one person.

Mortimer.

My druid friend now stands with his back against the trunk of a mighty oak. Set stands before Mortimer. The God of Chaos holds a sword. The tip of the blade sits right above the druid's heart.

"Answer my question," says Set. "Or Mortimer dies."

Questions echo through my mind. Is Set here? Or am I seeing another one of his chaos illusions? Even if it's probably a lie, can I take the risk that it isn't?

I look down at my pitiful spell. The sad little beams of sunlight aren't strong enough to do much of anything. How can I know if this is all an illusion or not?

A sad fact becomes clear. *I don't know what's real.* Which means Mortimer's life could really be at risk.

"I really don't know why Osiris befriended me. Cast any spell you like. This is the truth."

Set presses the very tip of his blade into Mortimer's chest. My friend screams. Worry twists through me. I'm a low-level warrior angel. I can't win in hand-to-hand combat with Set. My best chance is the incantation Osiris taught me.

And the light of that spell has gone out.

"Osiris allowed me to kill him," declares Set. "My brother transformed into an undead deity with the power of reincarnation. He left his wife and son behind in order to rule the underworld. And he abandoned you as well. Why fight me? And what did he hope to gain through you? You're nothing!"

He presses the blade a little deeper into Mortimer's chest. It's not enough to kill him, but his weapon is getting closer.

I can't lose another friend.

My blood pumps so hard, I hear my pulse in my head. Years of grief and rage breaks through. Something awakens inside me.

Power whirls through my soul. Before, a pale white light had erupted from the spell. That brightness is gone.

Another power takes over. My hands glow with golden energy, giving my skin the illusion that I'm made from metal. Particles of golden energy float up from my palms.

On instinct, I slam my palms against the ground. The rift in the earth seals up. I raise my arms. Particles of golden light flow from my palms, surrounding me in brightness that's so thorough, I can't see anything.

"Go!" I call.

The golden light becomes brighter than ever before. Then, it vanishes. I find myself back in my hut.

The walls are intact.

There's no sign of Set.

Which means my suspicions were correct. Everything I just experienced was an illusion. Mortimer stands nearby, whole and unhurt. He slams his staff against the earth while bellowing out three words.

"Who are you?"

3

XAVIER

Mortimer glares at me as he repeats the question. "Who are you?"

I lean back on my haunches. "I'm the same man you've always known."

"What was that spell?"

"It's one I learned from the desert realm."

"I don't mean your first spell. That casting didn't work. Then, some demon threatened me with a sword. Next, you cast a second spell with far more powerful magic."

Good question. Leaning forward, I examine the spot where I cast my spell. A few sycamore seeds are the only sign that I did anything.

"You want to know how I cast that second spell?" I pick up a few of the blackened seeds. "These ingredients must have carried far more power than I thought."

It's a good theory. Even so, some small part of me says that I'm missing something important. It all has to do with Osiris. As soon as the thought hits me, I dismiss it. Osiris lost his temper and fought someone he couldn't best in battle. There is no greater plan behind anything.

"Don't lie to me," declares Mortimer. "That magic wasn't due to special seeds. You've no idea what magic you wield. Which means it's not safe for you to live near my people. You spoke before about leaving. You are correct. Time for you go."

It's one thing to announce you're taking off for colder climates. Still, it's another matter to get kicked out of your own hut. That said, Mortimer is only trying to protect others. He doesn't believe in my story about the magical seeds. And he isn't wrong to doubt me, either. When it comes to the God of Chaos, anything is possible.

I nod. "I'll depart."

Scooping up my leather satchel, I stuff it with as many spell packets as will fit. All the while, Mortimer pins me with a disapproving stare.

In short order, I step outside, extend my wings and fly away. Wind brushes my feathers. The air is heavy with the promise of rain. Mist settles on my skin. As I go higher, the woods become a single undulating sheet of green leaves.

I can't help but compare this moment to when I left the desert realm. Flying away from Osiris' palace was like having my heart torn from my chest.

But leaving this place? I feel nothing but hollow.

Once I get high enough, I find a cloud that holds a different shimmer to my eyes. Humans can't detect this type of magic in the world around them. *I can.* In this case, I've spotted a cloud portal that leads to the desert realm. I fly through the spot. The chilly world of the Northern realm vanishes behind me. I come out over a great sea of sand.

The desert realm.

From here, it's a short flight to the Red Pyramid. I simply must inspect the place that's supposed to be keeping Set imprisoned.

More importantly, I need to check on the artisans who maintain the spells that regular Set's pyramid prison. In other words, my first stop must be the Sekhem village. That's where I'll find the lead architect of the Red Pyramid—a master of magic who keeps the world safe from chaos.

Please, let the lead architect be alive and well.

Sekhem Village

4

XAVIER

It's been too long since I visited the desert realm. What I thought would be a quick flight takes up an entire day. The hours pass slowly. My back aches with the effort of flight. The fact that I haven't slept in weeks makes my eyes sting and my mind wander.

It's sunset by the time I reach Sekhem village. I land outside a small cluster of brick buildings surrounded by a few palm trees and a lot of desert. I march toward the largest structure. That's where the lead architect resides, or used to.

As I step forward, I make a point of keeping my wings on display. Unlike some magic, humans can see my wings. Here, the locals will assume anyone with wings is a Child of Isis. Like the situation with Cernunnos and Mortimer, I'm not above allowing a misunderstanding to stay in place, especially if it helps me achieve a greater goal.

Like checking on Set's prison.

Someone runs out as I approach the town. He's an elderly fellow with leathery skin who wears a simple white kilt with sandals. Like most men here, his head is shaved.

"At last, a Child of Isis has arrived!" He wraps me in a big hug. "We've been pleading with the gods for help."

"I'll do whatever I can. Who are you?"

"Ah, I've been too excited for introductions." The man taps his chest. "My name is Kha and I'm the Lead Architect of the Red Pyramid."

A knot of worry loosens inside me. This is the lead architect. He's alive. That's a good sign.

"I'm so pleased to meet you." I gesture across my tattered robes. "You must forgive my appearance."

"I'm happy to have any Child of Isis here."

A deep rumble shakes the ground. It could be a minor earthquake, but those don't happen in this part of the world.

Kha grips my shoulder. "Did you feel that?"

"I did."

"The earth is giving us warnings. Set's power is ready to break free. The Red Pyramid will soon fail. I've made some improvements, but they won't hold for long."

"You're reinforcing the structure?"

"In a way. Are you sure you can help us?"

"Show me the pyramid. Whatever I can do, I'm at your service."

"This news lightens my heart." Kha gives my shoulder a squeeze. "And after you see the Red Pyramid, will you find Horus and ask him to aid us, too?"

I left my brows in surprise. Many humans have the name Horus. It's best to be sure. "Do you mean Horus the god? As in, the son of Isis and Osiris?"

Kha nods. "Stories tell us that Horus holds a never-ending banquet under the Nile. You are a Child of Isis." He gestures toward my wings. "You could go there and ask Horus for his aid. He's very powerful."

"I'm aware of those feasts." And I used to join in the celebrations, too. Sadly, after Osiris died, the parties became less entertaining. "Horus is powerful, but the way he entrapped Set? It was more of a fluke. No one expected him to retaliate, least of all Set."

"Still, Horus locked him in a prison before. He could do so again."

"I can certainly ask him." *And if he's sober, I may even get an answer.*

"When?"

"After I inspect the Red Pyramid, I promise to visit Horus."

"This is even better news! All the artisans leave for the Red Pyramid at dawn. That is the best time to see everything. You must spend this night with me and my family. Would you like something to eat?"

"I'm an angel… I mean, a Child of Isis. I don't need food. How about some fresh water?"

"That I can provide."

"And while I drink my fill, will you tell me all about your work in the Red Pyramid? You said you made improvements."

"Yes, come along. I will share everything."

Kha steers us to his house. It's another brick building like the rest in the little village, only his is filled with children. They rush about, pretending to be far too awake to climb into bed. I find a quiet corner and sit on a chair made of rough-hewn wood.

For his part, Kha fusses about his wife and little ones while pouring me a cup of water. I listen to the chatter of children, as well as the low rumble of voices from the village. More recollections appear. This part of the world hasn't changed much over the years.

Returning here is like a lullaby. Without meaning to, I slump against the cool brick wall and fall fast asleep.

Which is a grave error.

5

XAVIER

In my dream, I find myself standing in a strange room. The walls and ceiling are curved and gleam like silver. Strange acidic smells fill the air. I've never seen anything like this before.

Two men stand nearby. The first has brown skin and a lion's tail —that means he's a quasi demon from Purgatory. He also wears short white robes. Aquila's talked about these before; she calls them lab coats. The name Liam is written on a card that dangles from his neck.

The second man is a ghoul who's deathly pale with all-black eyes. He's dressed in a long black robe—that's the classic garment for all ghoul kind.

Neither of them are aware that I'm here. That's not so strange for a dream. They chat while using odd words like dark matter and quantum mechanics. My friend, Aquila, is an archangel who can journey through time. According to her, those words shouldn't be used for thousands of years.

Am I dreaming about the future? It seems likely.

"Do you feel that, Walker?" asks Liam.

The ghoul named Walker kneels down and presses his fingertips against the floor. His eyes widen. "I do."

"How long until the next breach?"

"Any moment now, we should—"

Crunch!

One side of the chamber buckles. Long talons break through the upper wall. Something's outside this room and it wants in, now. A jolt of awareness moves through me. I've seen those claws before. There's no question what's outside this chamber.

A tumult fiend.

This is a huge humanoid monster with curling horns, leathery skin and long claws. Like their leader, the chaos god Set, this creature appears to have been freshly-dipped in blood. Great roars sound as the tumult fiend tears through the walls. More red mist pours through the new opening before the tumult fiend leaps into the room and lands before Liam and Walker. He carries flaming torches in each hand.

I keep a dagger strapped to my thigh. Now I pull out my weapon and rush at the fiend. Sadly, my blade and body have no substance here. My blow merely passes through the creature.

For his part, Liam holds a dagger in each hand. Walker wields a sword whose blade is alight with white flame.

Both face Set's minion, the tumult fiend.

Tumult
Fiend

6

XAVIER

Liam and Walker take on the tumult demon. Both fight well. Given enough time, I'm sure the two men will defeat the monster.

In all the action of battle, none of us notice how more tumult demons have broken through the ceiling. These creatures pounce onto Liam and Walker, striking them with weapons made of fire and iron.

The two men die before me. There's nothing I can do to stop it.

A potent mix of rage and sorrow weighs on my shoulders. Although I don't know these two men, a fire for vengeance burns through my soul. Once again, I try to fight the tumult fiends, but it's like I'm a ghost. No one notices me or my touch.

More red mist rolls through the room. When it vanishes, the chamber is back to normal. Liam and Walker are alive and unhurt.

Was this all an illusion?

Or is something else happening?

Before I can think through the options, an oval opening appears in the wall. She steps through.

The woman in red.

Just as in my other dreams, she wears a red dress. Her auburn hair hangs in loose waves down her back. Her skin is exposed at her waistline. Without meaning to, I step closer, ready to brush my fingertips across her bare flesh.

Walker speaks, breaking me out of my thoughts.

"Camilla, you look beautiful," says the ghoul.

His words hang in the air. The woman in red has a name. *Camilla.* I turn it over in my mind and silently taste the syllables on my tongue.

"Thank you," says Camilla. She wraps Walker in a hug.

My stomach twists with jealousy. Walker's bloodless hands are touching her. Who is this ghoul to Camilla? And why do I care so much?

Camilla and Walker step apart. It's as if my lungs have been in a vise. Now, I can breathe again.

"That last chaos incursion was a big one," states Camilla. "Are you two all right?"

Camilla asks this question so casually, I wonder if these chaos incursions happen all the time… or if Camilla is the one launching the trouble in the first place. It's just like an agent of Set to enjoy what everyone else would see as a disaster.

"We're fine." Liam raises his arm. A silver satchel materializes in his grasp.

I've seen objects appear and disappear before. That's a basic spell. But in this case, it's as if the satchel has been cloaked somehow. Perhaps in this future, humans have developed their own kind of magic. Sometimes, Aquila speaks of such wonders.

"This has everything you requested," adds Walker.

Camilla takes the satchel from Liam's hands. It's a silver sack with a long strap that goes across the body. The object reminds me of my own bag, only Camilla's version has some kind of zigzag device to keep the satchel closed. Aquila calls them zippers.

Camilla opens the bag and pokes around inside. "My tablet is in here. Good." She pulls out a handful of small packets. These are like the ones I use for casting spells, only Camilla's version are wrapped in red papyrus instead of dried leaves. She holds up the crimson packets while staring pointedly at Walker.

"Is there a problem?" asks Walker.

"You packed way too many of these," says Camilla. "It's wasting space."

"Your symptoms will only get worse." Walker nods toward the red packets. "You'll need more as time goes on. Better to be safe."

Before Camilla's name had grabbed my attention in a good way. Now a new word—symptoms—is enough to make my heart sink. Is Camilla sick?

I scan her carefully. Camilla appears so vibrant and alive, I must have misunderstood Walker. What these people call *symptoms* could refer to something other than illness. This is the future, after all.

"In that case, I'll keep them." Camilla sighs. "Khrysonia is a bitch."

Now, I'm stuck on yet another word. *Khrysonia.* That's an illness I know well. Angels like me can fall in love with humans, no problem. It's different for archangels—their power is so strong that a true connection is poison. No one loves an archangel and lives. Even worse, their souls vanish from the afterlife.

My body turns numb. Camilla is sick with khrysonia. She truly loves an archangel. It might even be my friend, Lucifer. That man keeps secrets.

Closing my eyes, I make an effort to push aside all thoughts of khrysonia. This is some kind of trick. After all, Set already confirmed that he created Camilla in order to torture me. Perhaps she's pretending to be ill as part of her master's game.

This time, it's Liam who snaps me out of my contemplations. "Are you certain you're up for this?" he asks.

Camilla nods. "I'm the only one who can go after Xavier."

I recall what Set said in my hut. *Camilla is made to hurt me.* Now, this dream version of her is confirming his words.

"Is anyone else coming to see you off?" asks Walker.

"No," Camilla replies.

"What about your husband?" asks Liam.

"He's on a last-minute mission," answers Camilla. "Besides, I hate farewells. This is for the best."

A fresh thread of jealousy winds inside me. Camilla is married? I set the feeling aside.

This is a dream, Xavier. Nothing more.

Camilla sets the satchel over her shoulder. Once the bag is in place, it turns invisible again. With that, she marches to the center of the room and raises her arms. Columns of liquid silver rise up from the floor near her feet. The metal cords ascend to merge into a great spiral shape around her. It's some kind of machine. Aquila has told me about these as well.

The spiral begins to spin.

Camilla becomes a blurry figure in the center of a whirling vortex. Bits of silver fly off from the spiral to congeal around Camilla in a loose robe.

The structure moves faster than before. Walls shake. Bits of metal tumble from the ceiling. Liam and Walker shield their eyes. A mechanical squeal sounds at an ear-splitting volume.

The spiral vanishes.

Camilla is gone, too.

I awaken.

7

XAVIER

Opening my eyes, I find myself reclining on a wooden palette. Kha must have moved me to his own bed. Sitting up, I inspect the space around me. The room is a simple box with an archway for a door and a few wooden chests on the floor. Through the nearby window, I can tell that the sky is lightening. Dawn will be here soon.

Kha slips into the room. "Ah, you're awake," he whispers.

When I speak, I take care to keep my voice low as well. The rest of the family must still be asleep.

"Yes, thank you for bringing me here."

Kha motions me to follow him. We march outside until reaching a small cluster of palms that are located a short distance from the village. Here, we can speak freely while waiting for the other workers to arrive.

"How did you rest?" asks Kha.

"Well enough. I missed the chance to hear about your improvements to the Red Pyramid."

"We're almost there," states Kha. "Such things are better seen." He puffs out his bare chest. "I've enhanced the magic of Horus quite well, if I do say so myself."

I grin. "I'm certain of it."

As we wait for the other workers, I think back to my own little hut with its bundles of dried herbs and small bowls of unusual stuff.

Can't wait to see what Kha has come up with.

At last, twenty artisans from the village join me and Kha. Some carry chisels for smoothing out the rough stone walls. Others tote buckets of plaster in order to prep surfaces for murals. Still more of them lug containers of paint that'll create images and hieroglyphs.

It's a short walk from Sekhem village to a towering structure made of crimson brick. Unlike some pyramids, this one includes a columned temple at its base.

The Red Pyramid.

Here at last.

Red Pyramid

8

XAVIER

I breathlessly scale the front steps to the Red Pyramid.

Once inside, I find a huge room covered with intricate murals. *The Great Temple Chamber.* These images show Horus flying over the Red Pyramid. Beneath the structure, the mural shows a large black box buried underground. And inside that dark space is drawn an image of Set.

It's the story of Horus imprisoning Set.

Across the other walls, the remaining gods and goddesses watch on in awe of Horus' magic. Some pictures are chipped and in need of repair. Other walls are blank and must be prepped for painting. The artisans quickly get to work. Some fix fading murals. Others smooth down new stretches of wall for extra pictures.

I can't help but marvel at the ingenuity of humans. They don't have much in the way of magic, yet they maintain the Red Pyramid. And as they do so, each person knows their respective task.

I'm so caught up in seeing the artisans, I don't notice Kha step up beside me. "They are well-trained, are they not?"

"I wish our armies knew their work so well," I state.

"And their tasks have hidden benefits." Kha leads me to a line of paints in different clay pots. "See these?"

I lean in for a better look into the containers. Bits of cypress bark float atop the paint. "These are enspelled," I declare. "Protection from harm, if I'm not mistaken."

Kha beams. "Correct. We cast the spells back at the village and bring the paints here."

"And is that *all* the improvements you've made?"

"No, it is only the beginning." Kha gestures to the far wall of the chamber. The last time I'd been here, that panel has been covered in murals. Now, a doorway opens into darkness.

"Allow me to show you the extra passages and levels to the Red Pyramid," states Kha.

I grin from ear to ear. "Can't wait."

The back doorway leads to a thin passage made from red brick. The cramped tunnel loops down at a steep angle until it ends at a new doorway.

Kha pauses at the threshold and points upward. "We're right below the Great Temple Chamber now." He gestures toward the opened doorway. "This is the forest of the wooden hawk."

I follow the lead architect into what turns out to be a remarkably tall room. Like the Great Temple Chamber above, this place is covered in murals. Only in the center of the place, there's a forest of trees whose bark has been stripped. Atop the tallest branches sits a brown hawk in her nest, preening her feathers. And the bird is made from dark wood.

I rub my eyes, not believing what I'm seeing. "Is that bird enchanted?"

"It's more of an enspelled carving." A few boys in priestly robes stand by the walls. Kha gestures to one of them. "Gather up this morning's ingredient."

The child nimbly scales up the branches and pats inside the nest. When he returns again, the boy holds a wooden egg that's covered in delicate hieroglyphs. He hands over the little treasure to Kha.

"A hawk's egg is one of the ingredients for the imprisonment spell." Kha holds the wooden treasure high. "This figurine is enchanted to lay one egg each morning."

"Hold on, you don't just cast any old magic to maintain the prison under the Red Pyramid. You're using Horus' original spell, too?"

"Yes," replies Kha. "I found the incantation by chance. When the ground began to shake, I sought to redo the spell with more powerful ingredients." He raises the wooden egg as evidence.

I offer my hand. "May I take a look?"

Kha's lined face creases into a proud smile. "Of course." He sets the egg onto my palm.

The moment I hold the tiny object, a charge of power moves up my arm. "How interesting."

"We humans don't have much in the way of magic, so we must rely on enspelled ingredients."

"I don't have much magic, either. I'm in the same position that you are. Where did you the hawk?"

"It was created by the god, Khnum. We traded it for four sarcophagi."

I hand back the precious egg. "This is impressive magic."

"It is only the beginning."

Once again, we walk down a spiral passage to the level below. This time, the chamber holds a round bed carved from dark mahogany. A black hound rests atop it. It's a sleek beast with a long body and legs.

Like the bird, the hound is made from wood.

This time, Kha asks a priestess to gather today's ingredient. The hound waits while the priestess plucks the single fang from his mouth.

"The hound gives us one wooden tooth each day," explains Kha. "It's the product of another trade with Khnum. He required four sarcophagi this time."

With his task done, the hound sets his chin onto his paws and closes his eyes.

"He'll sleep the rest of the day," says Kha. "Producing a magical fang is rather taxing."

The priestess hands Kha the wooden tooth. The lead architect turns to me. "And what do you think the third ingredient is?"

"Mummy wrappings," I state.

"Correct. Allow me to show you the best improvement of all!"

Together, Kha and I step down another curved passageway to a third chamber. Unlike the first two, the walls here are lined with upright sarcophagi. All these coffins are brightly decorated with jewels and paint.

A half dozen priests stand nearby in white robes. One steps forward. Unlike the others, he wears an elaborate collar of gemstones. In his right hand, he carries a small golden dagger.

The moment sears in my mind. When I last saw the Red Pyramid, there was only the Great Temple Chamber. The lead architect used whatever ingredients were handy in order to cast a standard spell of protection.

Humans really are the most clever creatures. How can Set be close to such intellect, and his only thought is to destroy it?

The Great Temple Chamber

9

XAVIER

"Show our guest how you gather today's spell ingredient," orders Kha.

All the priests chant in low voices. All the torches dim. Minutes pass as the song continues.

At last, one of the sarcophagi swings open. A mummy steps out. Like the living priest, this one also wears a wide jeweled collar around his neck. The mummy approaches the living priest and offers his hand. Using a bronze dagger, the lead priest cuts a bit of wrapping from the mummy's palm. The other priests continue their song as the mummy steps back into his sarcophagi. The coffin door wings shut.

The room falls silent.

Kha looks toward me with his brows raised. He doesn't need to say a word. Kha's expression says it all: are you impressed or are you *very* impressed?

"Mummy wrappings are a key ingredient to many spells." I bow my head. "I've never seen a better way to obtain them."

Kha beams. "This mummy was obtained from Osiris himself."

The mention of my friend sends a pang of sorrow through my

heart. "You actually visited him in the Duat underworld? I thought only gods and goddesses could go there."

"Oh, we can't get close to the underworld. Osiris gave this mummy to the god Anubis. And in turn, Anubis gave us the mummy in exchange for four chests of golden rings, collars and arm cuffs. If you asked me, Anubis needs presents for courting. A mummy is no way to woo a woman!"

"True enough."

Kha turns to the priests. "I'm ready now." The lead priest hands over the bit of mummy wrapping. Kha then looks to me. "Ready to see me cast the spell?"

"Absolutely."

Kha leads me down a final spiral passage. It strikes me that each of these levels—the hawk, hound and mummy—are all stacked atop each other and filled with wondrous decorations.

The final chamber is different. This room has been cut out of rock. The walls are blackened with soot. There are no murals or magical animals to be seen. Only Kha and I are the only beings in the room.

A deep pit looms in the center of the floor. Crimson light flickers from its depths. I've seen Hell. This is different.

I round on Kha. "You actually opened the seal to Set's prison?"

"It broke open on its own," explains Kha. "I figured out how to contain it. The spell must be recast every day."

I lean in to examine the pit. "You can see Set's power below. And there's space between Set's onyx dungeon and the very floor we stand upon."

"Unfortunately, yes. There are layers of rock and dirt which separate this chamber from the one that holds Set."

"That must be where the chaos power seeps out."

"Not much gets loose, but over time? It is causing problems."

I nod. "Set used some of that magic to travel underground to my old home in the Northlands."

"That's quite a journey," says Kha. "Why would Set seek you out over such a distance?"

I sigh. "I wish I knew."

As if in response to my words, the ground rumbles beneath our feet. "Set is waking up," says Kha. "I must cast the spell again. Care to join me?"

"It would be an honor."

It's a reflex to reach into the satchel I keep over my shoulder. Indeed, I carry spell packets of ingredients that could help. But none of those ingredients are stronger than what Kha now holds. That said, I can still add my voice to the spell.

"What incantation do you use?" I ask.

"The imprisonment chant of Osiris."

"I know it well. It's one of his longer ones."

"Let us begin."

Kha and I move to stand by the edge of the pit. Together, we speak the words for the ancient spell.

We seal this room with potential.

As we speak the word *wisdom*, Kha drops the egg into the pit. In response, cords of red mist rise from the chamber below.

I check my inner magic. Normally, a spell will pull on my feeble angelic energy. This time, that's not needed. The ingredients Kha has pulled together contain more than enough magic.

Still, Kha wants me to join him. That's the least I can do.

Kha and I continue.

We lock this room with strength.

Kha drops in the wooden fang. More lines of red mist rise up. Kha and I finish the spell.

Through the power of lives past, we close this chamber for the future.

Kha releases the mummy wrapping into the pit. All the tendrils of mist retract into the dark. The crimson light below flares more brightly for a moment, then it dims to perfect blackness.

"The spell is done," says Kha. "Set is contained for another day."

"What you have built here is an inspiration. Thank you for sharing it with me."

"Let's go outside. This pit may be dark, but now that Set is awake? I suspect he listens."

Kha and I silently retrace our path until we stand on the entry steps to the pyramid. I hadn't realized it, but our journey took up the full day. The sun is already well below the horizon.

"Well, what do you think of it all?" asks Kha.

"I wish I could show other angels what you've built here. Many don't believe in the human ability to cast spells." *Mostly, I want to show Lucifer, although I don't add that part aloud.*

"Other Children of Isis are unaware of our power? Doesn't the goddess herself explain things to them?"

I could try to explain that angels don't exactly socialize with forces of nature like Isis. But I've tried to do so before. The conversation quickly becomes more confusing than helpful. Instead, I move onto a topic I know Kha will appreciate.

"Horus' celebrations begin after dark," I state. "As promised, I will see him."

Kha beams. "That will be a great burden from my mind. I believe that with Horus' help and our enhanced ingredients, perhaps we can fully seal Set's prison again."

I bob my head and consider this. "It's worth a try. Though to be honest, Horus is a little unpredictable."

"Aren't all children this way?" Kha sets his hand on my shoulder. "I know you'll convince him."

"I'll do my best."

"Now, I must return to the pyramid. If I don't check the artisans' work, there can be errors in their paintings. At this point, any tiny mistake may cause our work here to fail. Farewell!"

Kha steps back into the Red Pyramid. I make my way toward the Nile, which hides the entrance to Horus' nightly celebration.

I don't get far before I notice a strange object in the sky. It's not a shooting star. Rather, it's a slow moving orb that changes in color between orange and red. And the object is moving toward the Dashur Mines, a place where much of Egypt'a gold was uncovered. The place is now empty of both precious metal and people.

So why is Set sending a power orb in that direction?

I set my plans for Horus aside.

Best to visit the Dashur Mines.

Dashur Mines

10

XAVIER

Taking to the skies, I wing my way toward the mines. My back muscles soon burn with effort. As I fly closer, I get a better look at the sphere. The brightness keeps changing between orange and red.

This is what happened with the giant lizards. Set sent them death from the sky. A comet.

Is Set about to destroy all life on Earth again?

As I close in on the mines, I picture the spell packets in my satchel. Nothing I brought can fight a comet.

At last, I cross over the lip to the mines. A great valley opens up below me. The walls are tiered with rough rock. A small stretch of flat ground marks the lowest point.

My pulse speeds as I soar downward. Wind roars in my ears. Although my gaze is locked on the spot where I'll land, I can still sense the crimson orb getting closer overhead. The rocky expanse before me becomes cast in more intense versions of its other-worldly glow.

I touch down on the valley's lowest point. The breeze dies down. Chittering insects sound from tufts of nearby grass. My pulse speeds.

Looking up, I track the orb's path toward the ground. Every so often, it changes course. Each alteration is so the sphere will touch down right here, at the best place to land. I turn these revelations over in my mind.

The orb is changing its landing path.

Which means this isn't a comet.

It's something else.

Based on its speed, this mystery object should reach me at any moment. I reach into my satchel, ready to cast whatever spell may work best.

The light turns brighter. The orb closes in. As the object gets nearer, I discover that it's not an orb at all.

It's a spiral that's winding its way down from the clouds. The surface gleams with silver. Lights pulse along the length of the curling metal. I suck in a shaky breath. A realization appears. This is no orb.

It's the giant machine I saw in my dream with Camilla.

Perhaps that wasn't a dream at all. Did I really see the future? Or is this all an illusion?

The silver spiral whirls about, drawing my attention away from other questions. In my night vision, the metal spiral rose up from the floor. Now, the same shape whirls down from the sky. That must mean something.

The huge coil of metal moves closer. Inside the twist of metal and light, I spy a familiar figure.

It's Camilla.

Joy and rage battle it out inside me. Seeing this woman, even from a distance, lightens my heart so much, it feels as if I could fly without wings. Still, I suspect it's an illusion. *A trick.* Anger heats my veins.

The metal spiral moves even closer. Although the structure spins quickly, I can clearly see Camilla inside the metal coil.

From my satchel, I pull out a packet for a spell to dismiss a fast-moving illusion. After crushing the packet in my fist, I call out the incantation.

Scent and sight
Truth and light

A thread of magic moves inside me. Small puffs of white smoke rise from my hand. The strong smell of cinnamon fills the air. The spell is working. My vision clouds over as the magic settles into my eyes.

Blinking, I clear my vision and look up again.

It's still there.

The structure holding Camilla is closer than ever. Now that it's nearer, I can tell one thing.

Camilla is in trouble.

Camilla

11

XAVIER

As the corkscrew lowers, the loops of metal spin more tightly around Camilla's body.

Is this another illusion? Or is Camilla really at risk?

Back in my hut, my magic wasn't strong enough to counter Set's spell. At least, not at first. It wasn't until I accessed golden power that I could dispel Set's illusion.

Perhaps I can tap into that energy again.

Closing my eyes, I seek the inner power that once filled my hands with golden light. No such magic moves inside me. Whatever happened back in my hut, it's not taking place now.

Opening my eyes, I scan the spiral again. The metal loops now constrict Camilla. She arches her back while gasping for breath.

Alarm rattles down my spine. *This is wrong.* All the air is being squeezed out of her. The structure pauses far above my head. Still, it's close enough for me to hear odd clicking noises coming from the spiral. And I detect something else, too.

Camilla is screaming.

Her voice tears through my soul. What happens next is pure instinct. Extending my wings, I fly upward.

At the same time, I reach into my satchel and pull out another spell packet. While crushing the ingredients in my hand, I call out the incantation.

Speed of wonder
Strength of thunder

Magic churns through my muscles. My vision sharpens as I gain extra abilities. While flying into the spinning coil of metal, I claw through the silver with my bare hands. The coil bursts apart. Bits of metal fly past me. Everything explodes in dust and smoke.

The spiral is destroyed.

I fly about, searching for Camilla. The rocks and grass are only partially visible through the haze.

There's no sign of her.

Gasping for breath, I land on the flat stretch of rock once more. Smoke still surrounds me. Worry gnaws at my mind.

Could that spiral have been another illusion from Set?

Was Camilla even here?

Little by little, the dust clears from the air. I step about in a slow circle, looking for any signs of life. A weight of defeat settles into my heart.

She's not here. Even worse, I don't know if any of this was real. Despair weighs into my bones. I extend my wings, ready to fly away.

That's when it happens.

Camilla steps out from behind a boulder. She's perfectly safe and whole. Even better, she looks just as she does in my dreams. Camilla has ruby hair and a dress to match. There's no mistaking her full mouth, petal-soft skin and feline grace.

I could reach back into my satchel and cast another spell to erase any illusions. I don't, though.

This moment is too perfect to shatter.

Camilla

12

XAVIER

Camilla's here. Can this be real?

Part of me fears that I'm falling deeper into Set's trap. I should leave. Whether Camilla is an illusion or not, she's certainly fit and alive. Even if I don't depart now, I still can't ignore the possibility that Camilla is an agent of Set. At the very least, I should pull out my dagger or reach for a spell packet.

Yet, I don't reach for any weapons or magic. It's all I can do to watch her move closer.

She pauses before me. "Hello, Xavier. I'm Camilla."

Her voice is a lovely mixture of sweet tones and deep resonance. Normally, it's easy for me to grin and charm anyone, especially someone with a bit of demonic blood like Camilla. It's one of the benefits of being an angel.

Not this time.

I simply allow her voice to reverberate through me. A deep part of me awakens. In the place where my magic just felt hollow, I now sense the spark of golden power once more.

"Xavier?" she repeats.

"Yes, it's me."

A small smile quirks her mouth. "I'd know you anywhere, even if you do look different."

I scan myself. My angelic robes are rags and, if anything, my wings are dirtier than ever. It takes me a moment to realize the full meaning of her statement.

"You know me," I state.

"As you know me."

Camilla holds her arm out. A silver satchel materializes in her hand—that's the same way it appeared in my dream. Camilla opens the bag, pulls out an onyx-dark tablet, and runs her fingers across the surface. As she scans the device, it lights up with a series of symbols.

"It worked," announces Camilla breathlessly. "I've actually traveled thousands of years into the past." She looks at me and smiles.

At the sight of her grin, warmth floods through my soul. I want to bask in this heat, but I force myself to feel the chill of reality instead. Set is about to escape from his prison. Camilla is probably his instrument of escape. Perhaps I saw Camilla in the future, but that doesn't she isn't dangerous.

"The transport machine malfunctioned. I could have died." Camilla steps closer. "You saved me. Of course, you did."

Somehow, I ignore the adoring light in her eyes. "Why are you here?"

"We think of the past as absolute, but it isn't. If someone has enough energy, they can change history."

"Go on."

"I live far in the future. Something happened in the past—*in this very moment, as a matter of fact*—and it's pulling my present apart."

"It's Set's chaos power. His energy is breaking loose here."

"That's exactly what we think as well. Chaos power is churning up here and causing a chain reaction through time. Over in my reality, everything is changing. One moment, we're overrun with monsters. The next second, the world is fine again. The very fabric of reality is becoming unstable."

"That doesn't explain why you're here."

"I should think that's obvious. I traveled here to stop Set and control chaos." She points to the ground beneath her feet. "I must return to this very rendezvous point in five days."

I try to process this news. *Not happening*. "Five days," I repeat.

"Don't worry." Camilla holds up her tablet. "I have a countdown on here and everything. Until my extraction time, we can work together and stop this."

A foul taste creeps into my mouth. "Let me get this straight. You're a beautiful woman from the future."

"Thank you and yes."

"You traveled thousands of years in the past because you believe this is the best moment to stop Set."

"Right."

"And the person you believe can help you in this task is me."

"Of course."

"Huh."

"You have your *skeptical face* on," says Camilla. "There's nothing to worry about when it comes to my return trip. Walker will have it all fixed by the time I need to go back."

"I'm not concerned about that."

Camilla tilts her head. "Then, what concerns you?"

"Set told me to expect you. You arrived here in a manifestation of Set's power. Red is his color. It's all over you as well."

Camilla's eyes widen. "Oh." She looks down at her dress. "It seems I chose the wrong outfit." She shakes her head. "In my reality, this dress is your absolute favorite."

"You *are* beautiful in it."

"But?"

"Set wishes to wipe out all life on Earth. He told me that you're his agent. You need to tell your master that I'll defeat him, alone."

Camilla sets her fist on her hip. "My… master?" She shakes her head. "Who do you think I am, exactly?"

I straighten my shoulders and force out the words. "At best, a spy."

"And at worst?"

"A killer."

A long pause follows before Camilla speaks again. "Wow, are you ever wrong." She laughs. "I really came here from the future to help you stop chaos."

I rub my neck and think things through. "If you're truly from the future, then why hasn't Aquila ever mentioned you to me?"

Camilla shrugs. "Aquila is bat shit crazy."

I can't help but smile. "I'd be impressed by your knowledge of archangels. However, it's common knowledge that Aquila is more than a little eccentric."

"You truly think I'm a spy or assassin from Set."

"It's the most logical scenario."

She steps closer. I catch her scent. Musk and spices. "Why do you think I want to team up with you?"

"Set hates me because I was friends with his brother, Osiris. He doesn't fear me so much as wish to watch me suffer. You're part of his *torture Xavier plan*."

"So, in your opinion, I don't know you at all."

"This is not an indictment against you. It's me. I'm not a man who forms attachments, especially of the romantic kind."

Camilla narrows her eyes. I have the sinking suspicion that she's scheming something. But that could be another illusion from Set.

"Try this on for size," announces Camilla. "They come out at night without being called, and are lost in the day without being stolen. What are they?"

"Riddles?" I smile. "You're asking me riddles?"

She shrugs. "If you *don't* know the answer, just say so."

This brings me to a crossroads. I should fly away. After all, this conversation is probably another trap from Set. But, I have a secret love for riddles… which Set obviously divined and told Camilla about. I should not reply. Yet, I will. After all, I know the answer.

"Let's see," I begin. "They come out at night without being called, and are lost in the day without being stolen. What are they? Stars."

She winks. "Very good."

"My turn. What can you hold in your right hand, but never in your left?"

"That's easy. Your left hand, of course." Camilla moves nearer. "And I'm not in league with Set. You and I know each other in the future."

"How I wish that were true." I extend my wings, ready to take off into the night. Camilla steps so close that only a matter of inches separates us. I pause.

"You love battle," she states. "I hereby challenge you to a fight. If *you* win, I'll go away. If *I* win, you'll take me with you."

"And where am I going?"

"To fight Set and fix the Red Pyramid." She grins. "Come on, let's tussle. I'll even make the first move. I know that's what you prefer."

"I can't accept that."

"This is an official challenge. It's against your code to back down."

"I don't fight ladies."

"Here we go," says Camilla.

The next thing I know, we're kissing. As our mouths tangle, her body presses against mine. I run my palms against the bare skin on her back and hips.

I've been to Heaven. Touching Camilla is better.

Our kiss takes on a fierce edge. If this is Camilla's idea of tussling, I'm happy to take her on. She runs her palms over my neck and shoulders. I sense the barest pinch from her fingertips, but I'm too interested in her tongue to care.

Camilla breaks the kiss. "What do you say?" she asks. "Do I win or do I win?"

"No, Camilla. I work alone."

"What, today?"

"Every day, since the dawn of time."

She shrugs. "Alright, then."

I frown. *Is she really just giving in? That doesn't seem like her.* Only, how do I know what this woman is like? Chances are, Camilla is Set's illusion.

I expand my wings again. Camilla frowns. "Hold on. What's wrong with your wings?"

"What, I don't have wings in your so-called future?"

"No, they're different."

"How so?"

"They're… clean."

I may not know this woman, but I can tell one thing. She's lying. And I've spent too much time here already.

Pumping my wings, I take to the sky. I shouldn't watch Camilla as I wing away, but I do sneak a look or two. Back on the ground, she taps on her silver tablet.

An odd thought strikes me. *Is Camilla tracking me somehow?*

It's possible, but unlikely. Tracking spells don't use tablets, no matter what odd games Set may be playing here.

Best to move on.

I need to keep my promise to Kha and face Horus. Changing direction, I fly off toward the Nile.

And I actively ignore how sad I am to leave Camilla behind.

13

XAVIER

In truth, the Dashur Mines are walking distance from the Nile. But I don't want Camilla following me, so I take great pains to fly about in multiple directions. I avoid the thought that I'm secretly angling for another look at the woman of my dreams.

Sadly, there's no sign of her. *Such a shame.*

Eventually, I touch down by a deserted stretch of shoreline. Vessels float by with the Nile's current. Moonlight reflects on the shifting waters. Insects chitter nearby. Now that the moon is high, I can magically access the door to Horus' party from anywhere along the river.

No rush.

A foul taste creeps into my mouth. Horus' parties involve a lot of alcohol and pretending to laugh at his terrible jokes. I've always avoided them. And after the enjoyable conversation with Camilla, I've even less desire to spend time with anyone else, let alone a drunken Horus.

A human couple walks toward me along the shore. She is brown-skinned with even features. Like most ladies here, she wears a sheath dress, plaited wig and sandals. Her husband strolls beside her while wearing a white kilt and a carefree smile.

Clearly, they're in love. It's not something I've ever felt, but I know the signs.

I brush my fingers across my lips. *That kiss. Camilla.* I've never considered having a partner before. Suddenly, that seems like a great loss.

I can't help but wonder, *do these two have children*? Perhaps they return to a home filled with little ones, just like Kha does. For the first time, I consider having a child… perhaps a little girl who looks just like Camilla. The thought warms my heart.

The couple stares at me as they pass. I don't blame them for their curiosity. My wings are still on display, after all. However, the pair are far more interested in each other than meeting a Child of Isis. I wait for the humans to step off into the night.

And with that, I've stalled as much as I can. It's time to face Horus. With any luck, I'll convince him to sober up and cast another spell against Set.

This will not be pleasant.

Reaching into my satchel, I pull out a spell packet for opening gateways. I'm about to crush the ingredients when a figure slips out from the shadows.

It's Camilla.

And she's wielding knives.

Camilla

14

XAVIER

Shock skitters through me. *Camilla? Knives? I did not see this coming.*

Plus, Camilla has changed into dark clothes. Clearly, she carries more than a tablet inside her silver satchel. I should have guessed that, but I got too caught up in our kiss.

And the worst part? I know how Set operates. Camilla returning is another distraction that Set is throwing my way.

"You were tracking me." I shake my head. "How did you know where I ended up?"

"Not telling."

This is another kind of riddle. I simply can't allow it to pass unsolved.

"If I had to guess, the tracking mechanism was put in place when you scratched me." I brush my hand over the skin on my neck. Sure enough, I run across what feels like a slip of paper. I peel it off to find a silver square of fabric—an exact match to Camilla's satchel.

Camilla keeps her knives pointed at me. "Take your time. I'm only here with poisoned blades."

"Ah, here's the tracking device." I toss the slip of silver paper into the Nile. "That's a new one. Set is branching out into different spell work." I bow slightly. "And now, I must be going."

"Do not move."

I think back to Camilla in the round room with Liam and Walker. Back then, they all talked about Camilla being sick. I'd been worried.

Well, Camilla is definitely healthy if she can wield poisoned blades.

And since Camilla's master is Set? There's no question in my mind that there's something deadly about those weapons. It won't end well for me. I'm not the kind of angel who can heal from anything.

I slap on my best smile. "How about you put the knives down? We can talk."

"I've got the weapons. I'm leading the conversation. You're here because you want to join Horus' party."

"What makes you say that?"

"We have records in the future, Xav. Horus only held the same party every night for a few thousand years. Visiting him is a waste of time."

"What makes you say that?"

Camilla shoots me a deadpan stare. "Seriously? You're going to make me say it?"

"Say what?" *I shouldn't be enjoying this banter so much, but I do.*

"Horus is a pompous, drunken brat. His mommy taught him the spell to imprison Set. Horus did nothing but repeat the incantation."

"Meaning?"

"If we want to reinforce the Red Pyramid, then the person we need to see is Isis herself."

"I made a promise. I'm seeing Horus first."

"Well, I'm on a tighter timeline."

"Then, visit Isis yourself."

"She doesn't know me. You're coming along."

I purse my lips. "I don't see any reason why we must—" At that moment, the ground rumbles beneath our feet. I raise my pointer finger. "That's a regular earthquake."

"False. This part of the world does get earthquakes. *That* is Set getting loose and making my point that we must work together and fast."

"Says the woman with the poisoned blades." I sigh. "Much as I've enjoyed seeing you again, I'm off to visit Horus now." I shoot her another smile. "Are you going to stab me?"

Camilla bobs her head as she considers. "No." She flicks her wrists, making the blades retract into holsters that must on her forearms. "But I'm not giving up, either. I call for ceremonial combat again." She pins me with a hungry look.

Now, I could just cast my spell and head off to see Horus. But that really was an amazing kiss. So, I ask the obvious question.

"What kind of combat are we talking about?"

Camilla strolls toward me, pausing when our mouths are a breath apart. I cup her face in my palms and pull her in for another kiss. This one is a slow tasting. Heat pours through my core.

Camilla slides her hands up my shoulders. Everywhere she touches me, there's a trail of fire on my skin. She soon moves her fingertips onto the very spot where my wings meet my back. The sensation is beyond erotic.

Suddenly, a sharp pain zings across my shoulders. Camilla is pinching a particular spot on my wings. I'd felt a slight scratch when Camilla touched my neck before, but nothing like this. My legs turn watery beneath me.

"What magic is this?"

"Nerve pinch. It only works on lower-level angels."

"What? How?"

"I don't know how it functions, I only know that it works. You came up with this move during the great Hellscape Rebellion of 1632."

And with those strange words rattling around my head, the world around me starts to fade. My body goes limp.

I lose consciousness.

Barque

15

XAVIER

When I wake up, I find myself on a barque floating down the Nile. And the only other person in the vessel with me?

None other than Camilla.

Surely, this is all another trick from Set, the God of Chaos. I close my eyes.

Focus, Xavier. Think past whatever spell this is.

I take in a few deep breaths, reopen my eyes and take in my surroundings again. Sadly, this is no hallucination. I'm really riding in a fancy boat. On the Nile. And Camilla does stand nearby. She still wears her dark outfit.

Time to find out what's happening. I try to stand up.

Not possible.

Turns out, I'm tied up inside the vessel's bow. My wrists and ankles are looped over with silver cords. I've seen this kind of metallic fabric before—it's the same stuff that makes up Camilla's satchel.

This isn't the first time an enemy has tried to restrain me. Fortunately, I have a special skill for such situations. I can pop out my shoulders and wriggle out of most bindings. Slamming my torso against the vessel's inner wall, I force my right shoulder joint loose. Pain radiates down my arm and across my chest as I try to slip free.

It doesn't work.

Camilla has wrapped these fabric bindings around my arms and torso as well. I hate to admit this, but she's good.

"Good morning," I state.

Camilla steps over from the ship's stern. Even in a loose tunic and pants, she looks as beautiful as a queen in a formal gown. She carries her tablet in her right hand.

"You're awake."

"And you used a lot of rope."

She kneels before me. "Only because you can dislocate both shoulders when you want to. It's a trick you taught Harry Houdini."

"Harry who?"

"He hasn't been born yet."

"Ah, right. Because you're from the future." I meant for those statements to come out with more bite. Instead, my words sound a little flirty.

"That's right," says Camilla. "I am." Her gaze locks onto my mouth. Invisible lines of connection and attraction wind between us.

"Am I getting out of these ropes?"

"Not yet. I've been thinking."

"I'd say I'm not interested in anything you have to say, but it seems I'm stuck here."

"I'll set you loose, but you must give me your word we'll see Isis together. If she says we work solo, then I'll abide by her advice."

I bob my head and think this through. There aren't a lot of options here. "All right. I give you my word. We will visit Isis together."

"It's a deal."

After pulling out her tablet, Camilla runs her fingers across the device. Low beeping noises sound. All the bindings around me instantly fall loose. They twist together until they're all wound up into a small silver ball. Camilla scoops up that little orb and sets it into her satchel.

I rise and stretch. "How ever did you get your hands on a funeral barque?"

Camilla pales. "Oh, *that's* why this thing is so fancy."

I raise my right eyebrow. "You stole it, didn't you?"

Camilla nods. "In my defense, the little casket thingy in the middle of the boat is empty… and I left the owner a lot of gold."

"You came here from the future with gold?"

"Sure."

"Good thinking."

"Thank you."

Pain still radiates across my right shoulder. Reaching across my body, I gingerly touch the spot.

"I've been worried about that shoulder. You were tied up for a while with your wings still on display." She reaches for my shoulder. "I can help."

At this point, I should tell her that I'm fine. But the idea of her touching me is too delicious to pass up.

"Give it a try. Only, don't make me pass out again."

Camilla smiles. "I'll try." She steps around behind me and sets her hands on my shoulder. Her touch is firm and gentle, all at once. My muscles heat and loosen. "Better?"

"Yes." I glance over my shoulder. "How did you know how to do that? Angel anatomy isn't exactly general knowledge. We aren't like humans, especially when it comes to our back muscles."

"You and I designed angelic armor. It was pushing on that spot and hurting warriors like you wouldn't believe. We needed to redo everything."

"We?"

"We."

I love the touch of her hands on my back. "I want to believe you. But there's too much at risk. Set is a master of illusions and magic. He can cast spells that give you access to my memories."

"I know you," says Camilla simply.

"I don't pretend to understand how time travel works. You may know someone, but it's not me. I saw you in dreams. You love an archangel, Camilla. I'm the lowest-level warrior there is."

Camilla leans in until her forehead touches my back. The movement is so gentle, it makes my breath catch. "I don't know why you aren't an archangel, Xav."

A memory returns. I'm back in my hut, trying to cast a spell against Set. New magic churns inside me. Golden light shines from palms. Is that archangel power? Perhaps.

"Even if I do have some archangel power, then it's not enough. I'm a warrior angel, that's the lowest level in Heaven." I turn around to face Camilla. "I'm glad your Xavier is an archangel. Whether or not this is all an illusion, you deserve to love someone like that, although it does mean—" I leave the logic out there.

"So you saw that, too?"

My heart sinks. "I wish there were a cure for khrysonia."

"I'm one person," she says calmly. "There are bigger things to worry about here, like how to stop Set from destroying every living being on the planet."

"True."

A thin wooden dock appears in the water ahead. Other ships float past the spot. Humanity doesn't have enough magic to see the place, but they can still sense something is there. At least, enough to avoid a collision.

I point to the dock. "That's our stop."

Camilla and I tie up the vessel and march onto the desert beyond. Years ago, I flew away from these very sands in order to visit the Northlands and avoid memories of Osiris.

I never planned to see this place again.

Palace of Akhet

16

XAVIER

Leaving the Nile behind, Camilla and I march deep into the desert. A cloudless sky arches overhead. Fierce sunlight burns onto the sands and our bodies. As we leave the river father behind, the air turns so dry, I can almost picture the moisture wicking from my skin.

Camilla pulls out her tablet and brushes her fingers across it. "I have coordinates for the Palace of Akhet, but they don't seem to work for some reason."

"Isis and Osiris cast the cloaking spells on this part of the desert. No one can find the place, unless they already know where it is."

"How do you know the way?" Camilla shields her eyes with her hand while she scans the landscape.

"Osiris taught me the trick centuries ago. There's a slight rise to the horizon over there." I gesture toward the spot in question. "The Palace of Akhet is in that direction."

Camilla sets her tablet into her satchel and pulls out a gelatinous square. "Do you want one?"

"What is it?"

"Hydration cube. Set it in your mouth, it's as good as a big drink of water."

"No, thank you."

I can't help but wonder if she's still taking those red packets of medicine that I saw in my dream… assuming that vision was real, anyway.

Despite my better judgment, I can't help but ask. "How are you feeling?"

Camilla brushes her hand over her upper arm. It's an unconscious move, but an important one. "I'm fine."

I make a note of the spot. Camilla set some silver fabric on my neck in order to track me. Perhaps she has something on her arm as well. Until I pulled the cloth from my skin, the patch was invisible.

"This way." I march off in the direction Osiris taught me so many years ago.

As a step along, a thread of unease winds inside me. My instincts tell me to walk beside Camilla. What if she really is ill? It isn't easy to step on desert sand. She could fall and injure herself.

Set's warnings echo in my mind. *Camilla's a spy... my creation... she's the perfect tool to distract you.* Much as I hate to admit it, everything seems to be following Set's plan. And that includes how I'm buying into Camilla's story. Not to mention how I'm over-focusing on her.

At this moment, I should be considering how to approach Isis. Instead, I'm worried about Camilla.

After a short walk, we reach the right access point for the palace. I pause. Camilla stops beside me.

"I don't see anything," she says.

"Give it a moment."

Before us, the desert stretches out in what looks like unending sea of sand dunes. Waves of heat rise up from the sands. The warm air scintillates with magic.

One moment, there's nothing but desert in every direction. A second later, a great palace rises up from the ground. The building has multiple levels of brown stone decorated with columns and sculptures.

"It's beautiful," says Camilla.

"Aquila calls it *ancient modern*." I shoot Camilla a sideways glance. "Does that make sense to you?"

"As a matter of fact, it does," says Camilla. "This place reminds me of a series of long brown boxes that have been stacked together at odd angles. It's simple and lovely."

"The staircase to the main courtyard is to our right. That's the best entrance. You may want to wait at the base of the stairs while I go up and look around."

"Let me guess. It's the red hair."

"And the tail. You look like a minion of Set and—" I leave the logic out there.

"I get it. We know about this stuff in the future, too. Set killed Isis' husband, Osiris. I'll wait at the stairs."

I stare at her for a long moment. "You really trust me not to run off, don't you?"

"In your case, it would be fly off, and yes, I do. You keep your word, Xavier."

My chest warms with a sense of pride. The good feeling is shattered as I realize that my predictable habits—*like keeping my word*—are precisely what Set could use against me.

We soon reach the base of a steep staircase to the upper courtyard. As promised, Camilla waits. I march up the steps, alone. Perhaps it's the heat, but my mind plays tricks on me. I picture all the times Osiris and I walked up these same steps. My friend always marched with precision, even when trudging up a staircase.

Now, Osiris rules in the underworld of Duat. His famous chest tattoos are now covered in mummy wrappings while his skin is blue instead of brown. I finish my hike up the steps and reach the courtyard itself.

Nothing has changed here.

I look out upon a flat and open space that's accented by golden statues of Isis and Osiris. A pang of grief tightens across my chest. My friend should still be here.

I take a deep breath and refocus on the task at hand. Set destroyed Osiris. I won't allow chaos to annihilate the world as well.

Osiris

17

XAVIER

People stride toward me across the courtyard. As they close in, I realize these are the same priests and priestesses who lived here while Osiris was alive. The women wear shift dresses and plaited wigs. The men have shaved heads, bare chests and linen kilts.

I smile, remembering all these names and faces from years ago. The chief priest, Mezi, pauses before me.

"We didn't expect you back during daylight," he announces.

"Daylight?" I ask. "What do you mean?"

"Ah." Mezi chuckles. "We're pretending you didn't break into the treasury."

I'm not sure what Mezi's talking about, but that isn't so unusual. There are always strange things happening in the palace.

"I'm here to see Isis," I offer.

Mezi nods. "And you've brought an agent of Set with you."

"She's here under my protection," I state firmly.

"We understand," says Mezi. "No harm will come to her. We've invited her to join us."

Footsteps sound behind me. Turning, I find Camilla walking

onto the courtyard. She's accompanied by two priestesses. I'd expect her to be slumped-shouldered and worried. Camilla beams.

"Is everything well?" I call to her.

"I made some friends," Camilla replies. The priestesses lead her to stand by my side. "Guess we're together again."

My heart swells at those words. It shouldn't mean so much to have her back, but it does.

"You both must wash," says Mezi.

Camilla frowns. "Wash? As in now?"

"It's fine," I explain. "The priests and priestesses wash multiple times a day. That's tradition."

One of the priestesses bows to Camilla. "Isis knows you are here. She has granted you safe passage. We shall tolerate Set's pet."

Camilla smacks her lips. "Pet."

"No one will hurt you, daughter of chaos," adds Mezi.

"Oh." Camilla's tail arches over her shoulder. "I know you won't." She looks at me and winks. "It's bath time."

The priestess leads Camilla in one direction. Mezi takes me in another. As I expected, we end up in an underground bathing pool. It's a large rectangle made of brown stone and filled with chest-high water. After Mezi leaves, there's no one else here. A familiar line of pottery jars sits along the edge of the pool. These hold oils for cleaning up.

I strip off my rags and wade into the water. It feels beyond good to wash again. I take out my dagger and shave my beard. The oils straighten my hair and clean my wings.

A low gasp echoes through the empty space. Turning around, I find Camilla standing at the other side of the pool. She holds a linen cloth before her naked body. It doesn't hide much. All her lovely curves are on display. My blood heats.

Camilla stares at me. I know she's watching rivulets of water run down my chest. Fresh lines of connection wind between us. The rest of the chamber melts away.

The feeling between us is so intense and fast, this must be a spell.

But what if it isn't? Suppose Camilla really came here from a future stop on our shared timeline?

"You look different," says Camilla, her voice husky.

I extend my wings behind me. "As in, I look better?"

"Very." While keeping her linen sheet, Camilla steps up to the edge of the water. "So, we bathe in the same pool, eh?"

"Isis' palace, Isis' rules." At this point, I'm actually done washing. But there is no way I'm leaving. Instead, I slowly turn around. "I'll give you some privacy."

Camilla doesn't say anything else, but I do hear the whoosh of linen being tossed aside, followed by the splash of water as Camilla enters the pool.

I sense her come up behind me. "Your wings are in disarray. May I?"

If my blood was warm before, it's volcanic now. "Please."

Behind me, Camilla runs her fingers through my feathers. Every so often, she cups water on her palm and pours the liquid over my wings. Overall, Camilla takes her time and I allow it.

"Now dunk underwater," she orders.

I do so and rise again. This time, I spread my wings as wide as possible and scan them from left to right. "Everything certainly looks better from this side. How about from yours?"

When Camilla next speaks, her voice is low. "Much."

Little by little, I turn around. Camilla is neck-deep in water. Liquid distorts some of her figure, but not much. She's beautiful.

Camilla stares at my mouth. She's thinking about our kiss. I'm contemplating other things. I start to reach for her and stop. I only promised to keep Camilla with me until we spoke to Isis. Everything that's happening now? It's still exactly the way Set predicted.

There's simply too much at stake to get more emotionally involved than I am already.

I step backward. "See you in the waiting chamber." I gesture toward an exit archway. "From there, we'll process to the audience gallery together."

It takes an act of will, but I step around her. Her eyes burn into my back as I stride out of the pool.

Somehow, I'm able to walk away.

A grim thought hits me. If this goes well with Isis, I'm about to get a spell that will imprison Set forever. After that, Camilla will go. I'll never see her again.

That thought shouldn't hurt as much as it does. After the chore of leaving Camilla behind, facing the goddess Isis seems easy.

Isis

18

XAVIER

I wait in the reception room. It's a simple chamber with curved walls that are made of sandstone. Mural carvings show Isis and Osiris greeting other gods and goddesses when they come to visit. This is a room I knew about, but never used. My place was always in the family quarters.

Camilla steps into the room. She now wears a simple white sheath dress and looks radiant. For my part, I'm in a classic linen kilt and sandals. Although my chest is bare as is tradition, my hair is now long and neat. The one reminder of my previous raggedy look is my satchel, which I still keep strapped across my chest. No doubt, Camilla has hers as well, only it's invisible right now.

I offer Camilla my arm. "Ready?"

Camilla gently rests her hand on my forearm. Together, we process out of the waiting room and onto another wide courtyard. This one's also decorated in statues, only these are painted representations of other gods and goddesses. Isis stands before them all. She wears a beaded crown and necklace. Her golden wings are on display.

We process up and pause before her. I bow. "Hello, Isis."

"You bring one of Set's minions to my palace?"

This is classic Isis, by the way. The goddess chose not to attack my companion with a physical weapon, so she uses words instead.

"I'm a quasi demon from Purgatory," corrects Camilla.

Isis lifts her chin. "Why are you here?"

"We need information," I explain. *Best to ease into how we wish to fight Set.*

"No plans to steal from my treasury again?" asks Isis.

This is the second time someone has mentioned stealing from Isis. Set isn't the only one who likes to distract from the main point of any conversation. If I'm not careful, I'll spend my day explaining how I wasn't whoever stole from her.

"We need a spell to fight Set," explains Camilla.

The moment Camilla speaks, I realize she's the right one to state our purpose here. Since we're asking for help in imprisoning the God of Chaos, it's better for that request to come from someone Isis believes to be Set's ally.

"Osiris wanted to defeat Set as well," states Isis. "My husband believed he could gain new powers by fighting his brother. They did meet in battle. Set killed Osiris. And my husband did indeed gain new powers. Now he's the deity of reincarnation and rules from a throne far away from my own. Requests to confront Set are not my favorite."

It's tempting to point out that Isis can visit Osiris at any time. I cannot. But that doesn't get us any closer to stopping Set.

"Your son cast the magic to imprison Set," intones Camilla. "All we wish is for another spell to ensure that your child's work lasts for as long as possible."

Isis raises her right hand, palm forward. "Chaos cannot be controlled or contained, only endured. My son was foolish to cast that spell in the first place."

"Set has plans," I state. "He will cause far greater harm to this world than when he destroyed the great lizards. I can find refuge in Heaven. Camilla can go to Purgatory. This is your realm. Your fate."

Isis lifts her chin. "And I am woman enough to face it."

"All we need is a spell," states Camilla.

Isis purses her lips, but doesn't comment. I take that as progress.

"Or, perhaps you know a way to enhance the spell that the humans already use?" I ask.

Isis sighs. "Horus was too deep in his cups when he fought Set. No one expected it to happen. And in that way, my son out-chaosed chaos. That kind of opportunity will never arise again. There is no spell or enhancement that will work."

My mind spins through options. An idea appears. "How about a map of needing?"

Isis narrows her eyes. "That?"

I nod. "Give me a map that leads to whatever I need most. It doesn't have to be a spell for the Red Pyramid. The spell decides what is necessary."

"Now that makes more sense." Isis slowly steps closer to Camilla. "Because I can already tell what you most require. This one carries a deadly sickness. Khrysonia."

If Camilla is upset by this announcement, she doesn't show it. "I am ill. I have it under control."

Isis shakes her head. "Control and chaos. You two really are a pair." She folds her arms across her chest. "I will give you what you want."

All this time, a knot of anxiety has been twisting inside me. Some of that tension now eases. "Good."

"In the old crater beyond my palace, I have buried a tree of life."

"I know the place," I say.

"If you can summon that arbor and slice off a piece of its bark, that will serve as a map to whatever you truly need."

"Thank you," I say solemnly.

"What's the catch?" asks Camilla.

Isis blinks innocently. "Catch?"

Camilla pins her with a wary stare. "You know what I mean, sister."

"Oh, that tree is protected by the king of hawks," explains Isis.

I frown. "I've never heard of that creature, even from Osiris."

"Ah, it's just a large bird," continues Isis. "As long as you're swift in your actions, then I'm sure he won't gobble you up."

"Good to know," deadpans Camilla. *I'm enjoying her company more by the minute.*

"Now, I'm done here." Without another word, Isis saunters away.

I focus on Camilla. "I can escort you back to the barque, if you like."

"Hey, now. We have a deal. The two of us stay together until the encounter with Isis is over. And the way I see it, nothing is done until we have that bark map."

"I'm unsure." I scan Camilla, looking for any sign of illness. "Are you ready for this?"

Camilla chuckles. "Crazy hawks guarding magical trees? Count me in." Her tail pops up over her shoulder to wave at me. Camilla pats the arrowhead-shaped end. "I've faced far worse."

I can't help but smile. "In that case, let's go."

19

XAVIER

The so-called crater that Isis mentioned is a dip in the sands near the southern border of the palace grounds. I had no idea anything was hidden under that spot. Still, it doesn't surprise me that a magical tree is concealed below the desert. Isis enjoys hiding things.

Camilla and I reach the right place. It's far enough away from the palace that no one else is around. Reaching into my satchel, I pull out a spell for uncovering secrets and set that packet onto the sand. Kneeling against the warm desert, I speak the incantation aloud.

Break the thrall
Reveal it all

A little magic stirs inside me. The ground rumbles. Camilla and I lock gazes. The question is there, even if neither of us speak it aloud.

Is that earthquake the spell… or something else?

A few wisps of red mist wind up from the desert. A shock of alarm moves down my back. I lean in for a closer look. The mist to too light to tell if there are faces in the haze.

I look to Camilla. "I can't tell if that's Set's magic."

The ground rumbles more violently. Concentric circles appear on the sand. My pulse speeds. There is something hidden underground—and it's moving.

I rise and step back. It's a reflex to stand beside Camilla and rest my hand on her shoulder. Both of us watch the center of the undulating circle of sand.

Something breaks free from the ground. *A white branch.*

I exhale. "It's working."

Little by little, the branch rises, revealing more of the massive white tree that was indeed hidden under the desert.

"Check the trunk," says Camilla. "The map could be anywhere."

We move to stand on either side of the rising arbor. The branches are leafless, but the tree itself appears to be alive. And it is truly massive. The upper branches reach so high, it's hard to see where it all ends.

At last, the tree stops rising. We step slowly around the trunk, looking for something that could be a map. Sure enough, a square of the bark carries a slightly different texture than the rest of the tree. The hieroglyph for the word *map* is written large upon it.

"Here it is!" cries Camilla.

I always carry a dagger in a holster on my thigh. Now, I slip that weapon free, ready to slice out the map. Once the tip of my blade touches the bark, a new cry echoes through the air.

The screech of a hawk.

I cut the map loose. Camilla points to a distant point in the sky. "There it is."

Shielding my eyes from the sun, I take a closer look. "That's a massive hawk, all right. But it's nothing I can't out-fly."

After setting the precious map into my satchel, I extend my wings and scoop Camilla into my arms. We need to get out of here, fast.

That's when everything goes wrong.

Cords of red mist erupt from the sand by the tree's base. This time, there's no mistaking the ghostly faces inside the haze. *This is Set's magic for certain.* I pump my wings and take to the skies.

"Did you see that?" asks Camilla. She doesn't need to add the part about the red mist.

I nod. "Set is casting a spell."

The ground rumbles again. The skies darken. More red haze twists around the giant tree.

Crack!

With an ear-splitting snap, the tree explodes into a tornado of crimson mist. Faces scream and writhe inside the red cyclone as it speeds toward me and Camilla. Taking to the skies, I fly us away at full speed. The tornado of red magic follows us through the darkness. I push myself to go faster, but it's no use. The cyclone of red mist encapsulates me and Camilla.

It isn't easy to see, let alone breathe. Winds batter us around. It's all Camilla and I can to do hold onto each other. Red particles settle on my wings, making it harder for me to stay aloft.

All the while, the hawk's cries grow louder. It's closing in as well.

"I can't keep us in the sky," I call. "We have to land."

The tornado is so fierce around me and Camilla, I have no idea where the ground really is. I angle my wings so we soar down at what I hope is a safe angle. Camilla and I land in a tumble. Red smoke still whirls around us. I hop to my feet and check on Camilla.

"Are you all right?"

"Yes. You?"

"My wings are too heavy."

At that moment, the red tornado finally spins away from us. I see my chance. Shaking my shoulders, I try to clean away the heavy particles from my feathers. Camilla brushes at the same stuff.

"It isn't coming off," says Camilla.

Set's red tornado is no longer around us. Unfortunately, it's taking a new, worse path. A jolt of worry moves up my back.

"Do you see that?"

Camilla stops trying to clean off my feathers long enough to scan the darkened desert. "The hawk is heading right for it."

There's no need for her to say what 'it' means. The hawk is about to be engulfed in Set's tornado. I reach over my shoulder and try to slough off the red particles off. When it comes to chaos magic, you never know what will happen next. Camilla and I need to get out of here.

The red tornado encircles the hawk. I expect more crimson particles to settle on the massive bird's feathers. That's not what happens.

The tornado soaks directly into the bird's body. The hawk lets out a predatory cry as it grows even larger. Its feathers turn to molten lava. The bird extends its claws and lands on the sands nearby.

This animal was already a terrible predator. Now, Set's magic has changed it into something far worse.

And I still can't fly.

Molten Hawk

20

XAVIER

As a low-level warrior, I've learned that sometimes it's best to fight and cast spells. Other instances, I need to run for the hills.

In my experience, this molten hawk fits in the 'live to fight another day' category. That doesn't only apply to me, either. As outmatched as I am, it's just as bad for Camilla.

The fiery bird stalks toward us. The creature is tall as a mountain, molten as a volcano and angry as Hell itself. It rears its head back and screeches.

Camilla and I share a look. Once again, the question is there, although not spoken aloud. *What do we do?*

An answer appears at the same moment. When Camilla and I next speak, it's in unison.

"The map."

I pull the sheet from my satchel and scan it. "No good. The page is covered in scribbles."

Camilla leans in. "I can read it. This says something about burdens and freedom."

My eyes widen. "That's a flying spell. Osiris taught it to me years ago." After grabbing a fresh packet from inside my satchel, I crush the ingredients in my fist and call out the incantation.

Burdens of stone
To freedom unknown

My wings glow with magic. All the particles that had been weighing me down now disappear. Once more, I scoop Camilla into my arms and take to the skies.

The molten hawk also takes to the air. I push myself to fly faster. Heat sears my back as the hawk closes in. I need to get Camilla to safety.

An idea appears.

Angling my wings, I ascend. The hawk reels and comes at us, claws first. Pain sears on my leg as its talons slice through my skin.

I push harder and soar higher. It's a cloudless sky, so I can't find refuge by going through a portal. Even so, there are some facts of nature that can help.

The higher you go, the lower the temperature.

I pull on my inner angel power. My eyes glow blue with fresh energy. The skies cool as we fly higher. The molten heat on the bird chills, making it harder for the creature to move. I keep going faster. The hawk slows.

Another great cry sounds from the massive bird. Looking over my shoulder, I see the hawk transform once again. A moment ago, we were being chased by a molten bird. Now, the hawk returns to normal. Its molten body becomes feathery once more.

The hawk widens its wingspan so it can head toward the ground in a series of lazy circles.

Moments ago, I could only focus on flight and escape. Now that the danger is over, I notice how my leg throbs with pain. Changing direction, I search for a safe spot to land. The Palace of Akhet passes beneath us. I'm, in no mood for more chats with Isis. Instead, I fly past the palace and make for the nearby dock. Camilla's barque is still tied up, right where we left it this morning.

I land on the dock and gently set Camilla on her feet. "Set is a pain in the ass," she announces. "We really need to kill him."

I chuckle. "Two things about that. First, you don't kill chaos, you only contain it. Second, I'm not an archangel. Sometimes, the best I can do is make like an insect and flee."

Camilla shoots me a sideways glance. "Well said."

"Thank you."

Moving on," adds Camilla. "Perhaps we should check the map and see what it says."

I pull out the sheet and check it again. "It still only shows a bunch of scribbles."

"I can read it."

"And what miracle makes that possible."

"This is in your handwriting. Apparently, the magic of this map seems to think it's necessary to keep me around."

"My writing?" I lean in for a closer look. "I still can't read a word."

"Look, something very strange is going on here," states Camilla.

"Beyond the fact that you traveled through time to lock up a god of chaos?"

"You know what I mean. You're not an archangel… everyone at the Palace of Akhet thought you broke into their basement… and now, this map isn't just in some runes that only I can read, but in your future handwriting. Only the last bit isn't that unusual because you do have awful penmanship."

"Correction. Folks at the palace thought I broke into the treasury and I didn't."

"Oh, I thought of one more." Camilla raises her pointer finger. "You're right that Set could kick our asses. So why doesn't he?"

"Good question." I tilt my head and consider. "One theory could be that Set isn't at full power yet."

"And another?"

"I'll put it to you this way. Sometimes, a spell caster loses track of their ingredients. Let's say I run across some unknown leaves. Osiris taught me how to put the stuff through different tests in order to find out what they are. Apply this oil, that amount of heat and you know if something is poison ivy or mugwort."

"In other words, you think Set is testing one of us right now. My money is on you."

"Why is that?"

"The whole issue of how Osiris likes you so much. Set's his brother. That must bother him."

"You could say that. Set basically invaded my hut at the Northlands in order to lure me here."

"Good thing we have the map now. It will tell us what to do next."

I hand the sheet over with a flourish. "Well, what does it say?"

Camilla scans the sheet. "It says…" She scans the dock and gasps. "Hey, where is all that blood coming from?"

"Oh, that? I scratched my leg."

Camilla kneels down before me. "Your leg is torn. I need to fix this before we do anything else."

"You?"

"Me." Camilla raises her arm. Her silver satchel materializes in her palm. "I have supplies."

"I can cast a spell, too."

Camilla still kneels at the dock. She looks up at me with a stare that makes the molten hawk seem positively icy. "This isn't my first time nursing an angel."

Not too long ago, my biggest concern was being skewered by a molten hawk. In this moment, that worry seems like nothing.

A molten hawk has nothing on nurse Camilla.

21

XAVIER

Camilla reaches into her satchel and pulls out what looks like a silver coin.

"Why do I think that's going to hurt?" I ask.

She smirks. "Because it will."

"And what *is* it, exactly?"

"This?" Camilla holds up the coin. "It's a tiny bot that can clean and suture the wound."

"It's a spell."

"It's technology from the future." She nods toward her satchel. "Like everything else that has to do with me."

"As I said, I have my own healing spells."

"This is better than magic. It's science."

I tilt my head and consider. There's still a good chance that Camilla is working with Set. If anything, this situation is a good test. If this doesn't work, I know her true motivation. And I can always use my own magic if all else fails.

Also, there's no way I stopping Camilla now, especially considering how I'm still wearing the kilt from the Palace of Isis.

This can go in all sorts of good directions.

"What do you say?" asks Camilla.

"Let's give it a try… in the interests of science."

"Smart man." Camilla runs her palms up my inner thigh. There's a slight chill as she sets the coin against my skin. For a moment, nothing happens. Then, searing pain erupts along my leg.

I hiss in a breath. "That's the hurting part."

Camilla looks up and nods. "It's cleaning the cut now."

The hurt deepens. "And now?"

"Suturing the wound together. It's over in three, two, one." The pain fades.

"Now, you're healed." Camilla slowly rises. We stand a few inches apart. Fresh waves of heat and interest move between us. "Well, did I pass the test?"

"What test?"

"The one where you wanted to see if I'd try to kill you and thereby prove I'm an agent of Set. I told you, Xavier, I know you."

For a moment, I contemplate kissing her again. I set the urge aside. After all, we were just attacked by a molten hawk sent by the God of Chaos. This dock is far from the safest place to spend time. Not to mention the fact that Camilla is under the delusion that I'm actually her archangel husband from the future.

And if I'm being honest with myself, there's another factor at work here as well. The first and last person I really allowed into my life was Osiris. I'm still dealing with that loss. In the best case scenario, Camilla is gone in a matter of hours. There's no point opening up myself again.

"What I say is that we have more work to do," I declare. "I'll ask again. What does the map say?"

"You mean, you need my help here?"

"I do."

"And if I translate this for you, will you agree that we'll keep working together?"

As much as I know this may be a bad idea, I'm happy to be wrong. I lean in until our mouths are almost touching. "Yes, Camilla."

"In that case, it says the spell has three ingredients: an egg, some mummy wrapping and a tooth."

"Then, it's the same incantation that's already used at the Red Pyramid. What else does it say?"

"We should go after the tooth first. There's a handy picture to show who's got the ingredient we need. Even you can figure out who we need to visit."

Sure enough, the sheet has changed from nonsense writing into an image that I've seen many times before. "That's Thoth, the God of Learning."

"So, that's good, right? Talking to a scholar should be easy."

"Thoth is a character." I wince. "He lives in a crystal pyramid with his pet sphinx. No one visits him. Ever."

"Hey, it's a definite improvement from a molten hawk."

"Possibly."

"And where might this crystal pyramid might be located?"

"Thoth's pyramid lies beneath a stretch of black sand in the great desert. Everyone knows where he is. It's just that no one wants to spend time with him."

"In that case, let's fly."

We're still standing very close. And it is tempting to kiss her again, Still, it's enough to share this adventure together. I can do that without risking my heart.

Scooping Camilla into my arms, I extend my wings and take to the skies once more.

Thoth

22

XAVIER

Ever since I left the Northlands, it's been a series of odd occurrences. So far, I've torn apart a strange corkscrew machine that descended from the sky... fought a molten hawk... and confronted Set more than once.

But it's all worth it for this moment. Camilla is in my arms again. Her soft skin presses against mine. Heat fans across my chest where she exhales on my skin. My wings beat in a steady rhythm as we close in on Thoth's hiding spot.

The sand darkens below us. *We're here.* I spread my wings wide, making us soar in great circles and we head toward the ground. Once we're on the sand, I gently rest Camilla on her feet.

The desert is pleasant enough when flying high up. But this close to the dark earth? The sun is even more fierce. Camilla looks flushed. I keep forgetting that she's mostly human. Camilla needs rest, food and water. When was the last time she had any of that?

Camilla opens her satchel and takes out the map from Isis. She tilts her head as she tries to read my so-called scribbles.

"I've been thinking," I state. "This is a nice spot to take a break."

"Are you serious? Standing here is like hanging out inside an oven." Camilla scans the sheet. "Damn, this says the only time we can access the pyramid is precisely at midnight."

"So we have some time. How about I make us a shelter?"

"Don't you have a spell to force open closed doors?"

As a matter of fact, I do. Not that I'm telling Camilla that.

"The map says we need to wait," I reply. "That's what we should do."

"If you're trying to coddle me, it won't work."

I let out a hearty chuckle. "It's not you that I'm worried about. It's me. I just recovered from a terrible wound."

Camilla sets her fist on her hip. "Are you stalling to spend more time together?"

This woman. "Only a little bit."

She purses her lips for a long moment. "What kind of shelter?"

"Here's the thing. I have a spell that can bring my home in the Northlands this very spot, weather included."

"That sounds like pretty intense magic."

"It's nothing too tricky." *In truth, it's the most complex spell I know.*

I pull the largest packet from my satchel and crush it in my hand.

A spot that's safe
Where comfort abides
Bring my home
A place to thrive.

It takes a few minutes to pull out enough of my magic to cast the spell. At last, particles of sand rise up. The grains whirl around until they congeal into the form of my old hut. I pull the branch-door aside and gesture to Camilla. "Your room awaits."

Camilla curtsies. "Thank you."

She must stoop in order to enter. For my part, I make my wings vanish before following along—I don't Camilla to feel crowded in my tiny home. The moment we're inside, the temperature drops. A light mist drifts down through the breaks in my reed roof.

Camilla steps around. "This is an impressive spell."

"I'm the lowest-level angel there is. I have to do something."

Camilla sniffs a bunch of dried flowers that hang from the ceiling. "And Osiris taught you all this spell stuff."

"He did."

Camilla inspects different bowls of ingredients. "I have a question."

"Allow me to guess. It's the same question everyone has. Why did Osiris decide to train me?"

"That's the question."

"I honestly don't know."

Camilla leans her head back, allowing the mist to settle on her skin. "This is wonderful. Thank you."

"How about a picnic?"

"Why? Are you hungry?"

"Not at all. I mean for you." I sit on the pile of straw that serves as my bed. "Picnic time."

Camilla settles down beside me. We have our version of a picnic. It involves her consuming a hydration cube as well as a rather foul-looking nutrition bar. She starts to remove a red patch from her bag and stops.

"I saw those in my dream," I state. "Does that shock you?"

"Nothing surprises me about this week."

"In that same dream, those red packets turned out to be medicine."

"They are."

"If you need to take your medicine, then you should do so."

Camilla taps the red packet for a moment before pulling it out from her bag. She then does something I didn't expect. At least, not at first. She scratches at her upper arm and pulls off what looks like a strip of silver paper.

This is just like what happened when Camilla placed the tracker on me. The little bit of fabric looked like my skin… until I look it off.

So far, none of this is a major shock. Until I see what the strip of silver paper was covering.

The mark of khrysonia.

It's an unmistakable swirl that appears on the upper arm of anyone who develops a deep connection with an archangel. Sure, I knew khrysonia was an option. But it's one thing to suspect illness and another to see such as well-developed mark. Camilla has had the disease for some time.

My heart sinks. I'm not surprised that an archangel would fall in love with Camilla. She's extraordinary. But it is a tragedy that such a remarkable woman would have her life cut short.

Camilla rips open the red packet. Another silver strip of fabric sits inside. She sets the patch onto the khrysonia mark. Instantly, the fabric fades into her skin. Camilla hisses in a breath.

"Are you feeling ill?"

"I'm actually getting better. Every so often, the medicine from the patch hurts when it first connects with the mark." Her eyes flutter. "I shouldn't need another dose so soon. Sometimes there are side effects." She yawns.

"Come, let's rest." I lean back on the bed and guide her against my side.

"For a bunch of straw, this is very comfy."

"When you're choosing something to sleep upon, it's amazing how selective you can be."

Camilla yawns once more. "We should talk about Thoth. I know about the crystal pyramid and pet sphinx. What else is there?"

"I believe it is more important to rest."

"But I'm not tired."

Back at the Palace of Akhet, Camilla sifted her hands through my feathers. Now I comb my fingers through her hair. In no time, Camilla's breathing slows as she falls asleep.

And I do, too.

23

XAVIER

Waking up, I find myself back in my hut from the Northlands. It's raining outside and a gentle drip-drop of water falls through my roof and onto my skin. For a moment, I wait for the familiar footstep of Mortimer the Druid.

Then, I realize I'm not the only one here. Camilla still rests against my side. The sweet rhythm of her breathing is beautiful music.

The events of the day flood through my mind. Camilla and I came to the black desert to uncover Thoth's Pyramid. We need to take a breather, so I magically transported my hut from the Northlands to the desert here, weather included.

Camilla shifts and sighs. The sight of her peaceful slumber is something to cherish. I want to bottle every aspect of this moment so I can relive it later, over and over.

How many ages have I lived by myself? What's the number of mornings that I've awakened alone? Now that Camilla is here, I can't imagine dawn without her.

I recall Set from my dream. Ultimately, Camilla is an unknown entity. I'm not only risking my heart, but I'm placing the world at risk as well. I shouldn't be holding her right now.

Even so, I can't let her go.

Camilla stirs and looks up at me. Invisible lines of connection form between us. My left hand rests on her shoulder. Little by little, I slide my palm down her torso, guiding her until her chest presses against mine. It's a glorious weight.

Camilla shifts her legs so her knees lower and she straddles me. Fresh waves of heat move through my veins. I've never felt anything like this before. The sensation is simply too beautiful to end.

I slide my right hand up her torso shoulders and neck, pausing when my palm rests on the warmth of her cheek. Camila shifts to brace her arms on either side of my head, allowing the curtain of her red hair to fall around us.

Every corner of my being wants to kiss her. Still, it's a bad idea. She could be an agent of Set. Camilla leaves in a matter of days. And I'd be stealing kisses that don't belong to me.

An odd noise pulses through the air, like the chirp of a mechanical bird.

"What's that sound?" I ask.

Camilla sighs. "It's my tablet's way of saying that it's almost midnight."

"We have to go." I brush my thumb over her lower lip, loving the feel of her soft mouth against my skin… even while knowing I shouldn't kiss her again.

Camilla rises and pulls her silver satchel over. "I need to change back into my black gear."

I nod. "No knives this time, please."

She looks at me and winks. "They're not for you, Xav. I'm worried about Thoth."

Her words remind me of what we need to do next: face one god to stop another.

24

XAVIER

Camilla and I step out from my hut. As we cross the threshold, the air changes from chilly rain to dry heat. Once we're outside, the sands rise up once again to encircle my home. For a moment, there's a column of dark grains in the shape of my hut. The particles settle again. Any sign of the structure is gone.

It strikes me that losing my old home is more than the dissolution of a spell. Something in my life is ending, too. Another future is beginning. It's one that will be forever driven by these few days with Camilla.

Speaking of Camilla, she steps around with her tablet in hand. She taps the surface in a rapid rhythm. "Midnight will be here in five, four, three, two, one."

Both of us stand stock still. The silence is so complete, my ears ring. The clear night sky is pockmarked with countless stars. Dark sands stretch off in every direction.

There's no sign of the crystal pyramid that is Thoth's home. I focus on Camilla.

"What does the map say?"

"I'll check." She pulls the sheet from her satchel. "It's showing that same image of Thoth."

I rub my neck and think things through. “Perhaps I need to cast another spell.” I reach into my bag and pull out a packet of ingredients needed for spell of opening. “Perhaps this one will work.”

“Ha.” She winks. “I knew you had a spell to get us in the pyramid.”

I bob my brows. “I’m sneaky like that.”

Kneeling down, I set the packet against the dark sands and whisper the incantation.

Open the way
Reveal the day

It takes time, but I’m able to drag a little magic out of my soul. The edges of the packet brighten and curl as if the paper were on fire. Next, the charred ingredients sink into the ground. Long moments pass. I’m about to try another spell when it happens.

The sands give way beneath us.

Camilla and I sink into the ground and fast. As we tumble through the earth, pure darkness surrounds us.

Moments later, we land in a massive cavern. All around, the ground is paved with huge stones. In the center of the space, there stands a raised platform. And atop that massive stage? There sits a glowing pyramid that’s made of white crystal.

Camilla steps closer to the pyramid. The light from the crystal surrounds her body, casting her in a supernatural glow. She glances at me over her shoulder.

“This is it.”

And she’s right.

Thoth's Pyramid

25

XAVIER

I take a moment to soak in my surroundings. A low hum sounds. The scent of burning oil fills the air. Far up in the cavern's ceiling, I notice a dark hole in the sheet of rock.

That's where we fell through. Good to know.

I turn my attention toward the pyramid itself. Tiny lights dance within the crystal.

"This seems like your territory," I state.

Camilla sends me a sideways glance. "Mine?"

"This pyramid looks like something from the future."

"Ah." Camilla purses her lips. "If I had to guess, I'd say this crystal is a power source."

"Thoth is known as an inventor. It makes sense that he'd want some way to drive his creations." I step closer to the crystal pyramid, ready for a closer look. As I step nearer, something unexpected happens.

A door swings open within the rocky base that holds the pyramid.

Camilla gestures toward the new entrance. "Do you get the feeling someone's listening in our conversations?"

"For a while now. Let's see where this leads."

Together, Camilla and I march across the threshold and into a huge tunnel that's made from the same white crystal as the pyramid. The walls light up as we march along. Once we've walked a while, a sheet of silver fabric falls behind us, covering our retreat.

I gesture toward the metallic barrier. "That looks like the same material as your satchel."

"Someone's closing off the tunnel in segments. It reminds me of a clean room."

"Clean room?" I repeat. "Aquila hasn't mentioned that one."

"It's a way of sealing off the air and particles in a specific place. If I had to guess, Thoth wants to keep something out."

"Or in," I add.

More of the tunnel lights up before us. The message is clear if unspoken: *step along this path.* We follow the wide tunnel as it leads deeper underground. Every so often, a sheet of silver fabric falls behind us, sealing us in.

"Did Osiris ever mention Thoth to you?" asks Camilla.

"Nothing more than what I've told you."

As we trudge forward, the tunnel keeps lighting up in the distance, showing us where to go. Hours pass as this sequence repeats. All of which is why it's a shock when the tunnel splits into two channels. The left passage is dark. The right way is brighter.

Camilla and I reach the break in the tunnel. Turns out, there's a reason why the left channel is in shadows. A massive creature sleeps in that hallway. It has the body of a lion and the face of a man with a pharaonic headdress. The creature rests its chin rests on its forepaws. Its gentle snores echo through the passage.

It's Thoth's pet, the Sphinx.

Turning to Camilla, I mime my fingers walking toward the animal. I lift my brows. *Should we go in for a closer look?*

Camilla bobs her head and considers before pulling up the map again. The image is the same. The sheet shows the image of Thoth, not the Sphinx. She mimes her fingers walking away. I nod.

Leaving the Sphinx behind, we follow the pathway as it winds lower. A few times, I'm tempted to make my wings materialize so we can fly forward at a faster rate. After all, the hallway is certainly wide enough to accommodate me. But seeing the Sphinx reinforces the decision to walk. If we go too quickly through these tunnels, we could run into trouble without meaning to do so.

At last, the glowing tunnel ends in a square wall. As we close in on the spot, a small door swings open at the base. Like the rest of the structure, the door is made from the same glowing white crystal.

Camilla and I share a long look and a slow smile.

This is it. Thoth.

26

XAVIER

Camilla and I pass through the doorway and into a large chamber. This time, it's as if we've stepped *inside* another crystal pyramid—all the walls and floor glow with white light. Other than that, the chamber appears to be empty, with one exception.

Thoth.

He stands eight feet tall with the body of a man and the head of an ibis bird. He holds a tablet in his hands. The device reminds me of the one Camilla uses, only Thoth's version is made from white crystal.

The god looks up as we enter. "Camilla! Xavier! So nice of you to visit. I just have a few questions for you." Despite having such a long and curved beak, he speaks clearly.

"Questions?" I frown. "About what, exactly?"

"About Set's chaos power." Thoth steps up to Camilla. A light shines out from the back of his tablet casting a grid pattern onto her body. "According to my body scan, you have none of Set's power on you."

"Uh, thanks," says Camilla.

Thoth does the same thing to me. The light is so searingly bright, it's a reflex to cover my eyes with my hand. "You're clear as well," announces Thoth.

Once in a while, Osiris would take on the head of a hawk during a conversation. Somehow, that change never grabbed my attention. But watching Thoth speak is fascinating.

"And why do you care about Set's magic?" I ask.

"I'm a wise man who plans for all contingencies. This is all about preparation."

My eyes widen. "You're worried about Set destroying the Earth. Only you aren't trying to stop him, you're planning to continue living down here."

Camilla nods. "That's why you sealed off the tunnel along the way. You want to see if you can stop Set's magic from following us in."

Thoth nods. "And I've succeeded. Set's power has been following you everywhere but here. Thank you for your help in confirming my eternal security. You may leave now."

"Not so fast," I state. "We've done something for you. Now, we need something as well."

This is how it works with Osiris and the other forces of nature. There must always be a trade.

Thoth keeps tapping on his tablet. "And what do you wish?"

"We're looking for a magical tooth. It will be used in a spell to contain Seth."

"Contain chaos?" Thoth laughs. The sound reminds me of the high-pitched twitter of a bird. "That's impossible. You're wasting your time. Isis agrees with me."

"Yet, Horus disagrees," I state. "And his spell has kept Set contained under the Red Pyramid for years. That means something."

Thoth taps away at double speed. "Isis sits in the Palace of Akhet and waits for her demise. Horus drinks himself stupid in a never-ending celebration under Nile. I'm planning to continue my existence in isolation. You can judge who's the wisest of us three."

Camilla leans in close. When she speaks, it's in a voice that only I can hear. "We could waste hours trying to convince Thoth that he's wrong. I don't think it will make much difference."

"Agreed." Raising my voice, I address Thoth again. "It doesn't change the fact that we've done you a service. We wish a magical tooth in payment. I have a map from Isis which says you can provide this to us. Once this item is delivered, we'll go."

"I've one more question first." Thoth looks up from his tablet. "This is you you, Xavier."

I've a pretty good idea what Thoth is about to ask, but I still want to hear the question. "What do you wish to know?"

"After the War of the Clouds, Osiris plucked you from the battlefield. It's a curious choice. Osiris was obsessed with controlling the chaos of his brother, Set. Why save a useless angel? No offense."

I shrug. "None taken."

"For a time, I thought you might be helpful in the fight against Set, perhaps in some unexpected way. But seeing you now? It's clear you couldn't possibly be any help."

I think back to the Northlands. Back in my hut, some strange golden magic appeared on my hands. Yet, even if that power is real, I never manifested it while Osiris was alive.

Thoth lifts his beak. "Well, am I wrong, Xavier?"

"I don't know why Osiris chose me. Perhaps he has a little chaos magic inside him, same as Set."

"No, that's wrong," says Thoth simply. "Osiris is more calculating than I am. If he chose you, it was for a reason. I just can't imagine what it might be."

Every time we meet another deity, it's clear that my friendship with Osiris was some kind of group mystery.

Thoth refocuses on his tablet. "That is all." He starts to walk away.

"What about the tooth?" asks Camilla.

"Ah." Thoth makes a movement as if smacking his lips, only the motion is more like clacking his beak. "You can pick up the magical tooth on your way out."

"Thank you," I state. "Where is it?"

"In the Sphinx's mouth. You can remove a fang rather easily." Thoth steps across the room. Another door opens in the far wall. In short order, Thoth steps through it and is gone.

The lights in the great pyramid chamber dim. A door opens behind us—it's the same one that Camilla and I used to get in here.

Again, the meaning is clear. *You can exit this way.*

I wince. "This isn't what I expected."

Camilla grins. "Steal a tooth from a sleeping Sphinx? This'll be fun."

I lean in for a closer look. Camilla really is excited. "What kind of quasi demon are you, exactly?"

"Each of my kind has magic that aligns to one of the deadly sins. I'm a special case. I have two powers: lust and wrath." Camilla's tail arches over her shoulder as she adds a final thought.

"My people love a good fight."

27

XAVIER

Camilla and I leave through the same network of tunnels that we used to enter. Every so often, silver fabric lowers behind us, sealing the passage behind us..

Now that I know what Thoth is planning, the fabric seems more pathetic than futuristic. How can Thoth hope to live down here for all eternity while the rest of earth is destroyed? And even if he can do so, would that kind of existence even be worthwhile?

We soon reach the break in the tunnels. Sure enough, the Sphinx is still there and deep in sleep.

I extend my wings and fly a few feet into the air. The Sphinx sniffs and stirs. Not that I blame the creature for getting alerted. I essentially just wafted my scent at him. I land on the tunnel floor again, turn to Camilla and shrug. *What should we do?*

Camilla mimes climbing. I sigh and consider the idea. Between the two of us, Camilla is much smaller. She has the better chance of scaling up the creature without being detected. I just hate the idea of her getting closer to danger, that's all.

I wince and shake my head. *Bad idea.*

Camilla taps her chest. *I'm going anyway.*

Sadly, I can't think of a better plan. Besides, Camilla has

certainly proven herself to be quick witted and resourceful. I nod and force a smile. *You can do this.*

Camilla slips toward the Sphinx. As I watch her go, I keep my wings extended, just in case I need to grab her and make a quick getaway.

Camilla steps up to front paw. She sets her palm on the Sphinx's fur. The creature doesn't stir. Camilla puts her second hand in place and hoists herself up to stand on the Sphinx's front paw. The animal still snores away. I'm glad someone here is calm enough to rest. My heart is beating so quickly, I worry it might break through my rib cage.

Camilla glances over her shoulder at me and winks. *This woman.*

The Sphinx keeps resting with its chin on its front paws. Camilla sidesteps along the creature's front leg until she stands before its human face. Fresh ropes of anxiety twist inside me.

Camilla scooches closer to the Sphinx's mouth. Little by little, she moves its upper lip to expose a golden fang. Camilla grasps the tooth and slowly wriggles it free.

Each time the tooth shifts, something inside me screams, *This is the moment the Sphinx will awaken!* Each time, it stays asleep.

Camilla fully pulls out the tooth. Some worry eases from my body. Gripping the fang in her left hand, Camilla scales her way back down the creature's front leg. She silently lands on the floor. I smile so hard, my face hurts.

Moving as quietly as possible, I wrap her in a quick hug. Together, we tiptoe away from the Sphinx. We're almost at the turn to the main passageway when it happens. A deep voice echoes all around us.

"You must pay me for what you've stolen. Your debt can be settled by answering my riddle… or by forfeiting your lives."

Wincing, I look over my shoulder. The Sphinx is wide awake.

No question what to say here.

"Riddle," I state.

"Agreed," adds Camilla.

The Sphinx moves into a sitting position. "What gets broken without being held?"

Camilla and I lock gazes. The tight lines of her face loosen with relief. She knows the answer, same as I do.

"A promise," we reply.

"Well said," declares the Sphinx. "But, I'll kill you anyway."

A charge of energy moves through me. My eyes blaze with blue light. I scoop Camilla into my arms, extend my wings, and fly off at full speed. The Sphinx lopes along for a few strides before its own wings extend.

Camilla looks over my shoulder. "Wings? Since when does a Sphinx fly?"

"Not to worry. The Sphinx is a bulky creature. We can beat it out of here."

That's when I see the first silver barrier.

"Houston, we have a problem," says Camilla.

I'm not exactly sure what that means, but I understand enough. "There's a dagger on my thigh," I tell Camilla. "Can you use it to slice through?"

"I've got something better. I just need to change position."

"While I fly at full speed, Camilla moves so we're chest to chest. She locks her legs around my hips and her right arm around my neck. I loop my arms around her waist.

"Give me a countdown when we're close," calls Camilla.

"As you command."

Things are happening too quickly for a lot of strategic thought. At this point, I know Camilla has a plan. That's enough for me. The first barrier approaches. I give the countdown.

"Three, two, one!"

Camilla's tail juts forward. With one swift movement, her tail slices through the barrier like it's paper. We fly through.

"What did you say your tail is covered in again?"

"I didn't. It's dragon scales."

I smile and squeeze Camilla more tightly against me. *We're doing this. It's working.*

Another voice sounds in the hallway. "You're ruining everything. Stop breaking my seals! Chaos can get in now!"

That would be Thoth.

And I'm ignoring him entirely. Instead of responding, I push myself to fly faster than ever before. We break through seal after seal until reaching the main chamber. I head straight for the hole in the roof.

Camilla sees where we're headed, same as I do. "That passage is too small. You can't use your wings."

"We were magically pulled down here. Let's hope the spell works both ways."

Camilla grabs onto me more closely. "I'm hoping."

For my part, I keep flying at top speed. At the last moment, I retract my wings against my back. Momentum keeps me and Camilla moving into the exit passage. A sense of weightlessness takes over, but is it inertia or the spell?

The answer comes when we're both drawn back up toward the Earth's surface. The moment we burst through the sand, I extend my wings again and take to the sky. I don't hear Thoth or the Sphinx behind us, but I won't make the mistake of waiting around for them, either. We've other work to do if we're going to stop Set.

"Where do we get the next ingredient?" I ask.

Camilla shimmies about as she checks the map in her satchel. Throughout her movements, I keep my arms safely wrapped around her waist.

"The map says we can get the egg from someone called Sobek," replies Camilla. "I hope that means something to you."

"Sobek lives in an oasis temple that's not far from here." I give her waist another squeeze. "Is this position acceptable?"

She nuzzles my ear. "Very."

We soar through the air with our magical treasure. the most compelling woman in all history is with me. In this moment, I wish I could really be Camilla's Xavier. Instead, I'll have to settle for sharing this adventure with her.

It's something I'll savor for the rest of my life.

Sobek

28

XAVIER

I fly us deep into the Southern realm. Soon, the deserts give way to swaths of palm trees that are heavy with dates. Small ponds dot the landscape. The scent of fresh lilies fills the air.

Even within this verdant land, Sobek has created an especially welcoming home. He calls it his oasis. It's a series of low buildings framed by tall columns and pools of fresh water. Everything is painted in bright colors.

I extend my wings so Camilla and I land by the largest pool. The place isn't deserted so much as quiet. There's still a sense of life and joy here, even if someone doesn't rush out to greet us.

Camilla slowly lowers her legs from around my waist. "That was interesting."

I tilt my head. "Do you need to rest?"

"Not after an adventure." She brushes a gentle kiss across my lips.

I've spent my many years on earth protecting humans. I keep them away from demons and trouble. It never occurred to me that one might find it exciting to face off against monsters.

And Camilla leaves in a matter of hours. *What will I do without her?*

Our gazes lock. Just days ago, Camilla became a reality in my life. Ever since then, a quiet voice in the back of my head has been warning me about her. *Spy. Killer. Distraction.* And there's another factor I need to consider.

She's not mine.

Camilla quirks a smile. "What's going on in that handsome noggin of yours, Xavier?"

Fortunately, I've spent enough time with Aquila to understand what Camilla means here. The response is obvious. Unfortunately, Camilla won't like it.

I take in a long breath. "I'm not your Xavier."

When Camilla next speaks, her voice takes on a biting edge. "Yes, you are."

"You're not thinking clearly, Camilla."

"No." Camilla steps back. Her tail arches over her shoulder so that the arrowhead-shaped end points at me. "I know you, Xavier. I. Know. You."

A new voice fills the air. "Greetings, my friends!"

The speaker soon becomes obvious as Sobek steps out from behind a nearby pillar. Like Thoth, he stands eight feet tall. His body is lean, dark and topped with the head of a crocodile. Also like Thoth, he has no problem speaking through his extended mouth. He also wears a long robe that reminds me of Mortimer the Druid.

As Sobek approaches, he throws his arms open wide. "I am so happy to have you both here. Xavier the angel and Camilla, the daughter of Purgatory. I've heard of your quest from Isis. I hope you can stay for a long visit."

"Thank you," I state. "We appreciate your generous offer, but we need to get an ingredient for a spell. After that, we must leave."

"Ah, you wish to ensure that Set stays under the Red Pyramid." Sobek claps his hands. "It's a worthy cause that's best discussed after dinner, don't you agree?"

"Dinner?" asks Camilla.

"Do not worry," adds Sobek. "I have the tastiest breads and dates. You'll enjoy this meal."

Camilla smiles. "I'm sure I will."

"First, allow my people to lead you to your rooms. I'm sure you wish to wash up and change before the meal." Sobek claps his hands again. Priests and priestesses step out from a nearby building. Like Sobek, they all wear long green robes. They are all human in form with one exception: their skin carries the bumpy texture of a crocodile's.

The priestesses encircle Camilla. Protective energy runs through my body. I round on Sobek. "I don't like the idea of being separated."

"You are both safe here." Sobek ticks his finger from side to side. "And this is not the Palace of Akhet. Men and women stay in separate compounds. But do not worry. You'll meet up soon enough for dinner."

After our experiences with Thoth, I'm a little wary of being separated from Camilla. Still, Osiris always spoke kindly of Sobek. And we certainly do need his help. Plus, Camilla has already proven she can take care of herself.

"All right." I bow slightly at the waist. "Thank you for your hospitality."

Sobek shoos away the priests. "Go on and prepare for the feast. I'll show Xavier to his rooms myself."

We walk through a series of low buildings and wide pools until Sobek brings me to a little brick house painted in bright colors. Inside, there's a small bathing pool set into the floor. The room also contains some chairs as well as a wooden bed. It's like I'm back in the palace with Osiris.

"This is so kind of you," I state.

"It is a trifle. Please take some ease before dinner. My priests will come for you at sunset."

Sobek strides away, leaving me alone in the room. I take a long bath and a short nap. All the while, I try not to think about Camilla. Still, questions fill my mind.

What is she doing now?

Has she accepted the truth of who I am?

What is *her* Xavier thinking, wherever he is?

Camilla's true mate must love her at least as much as I do. The idea of causing her pain and death must be unbearable for him. How powerless he must feel. And even though I don't know the man, I pity him deeply. He's had more time with my Camilla. His agony must be far sharper.

Before I know it, the priests have returned and it's time for dinner.

And I will see Camilla again.

Sobek's Oasis

29

XAVIER

Sobek's priests lead me into a long chamber with brightly-painted walls and many columns. In the center of the room, there lie piles of pillows and blankets. Sobek is already there, sitting cross-legged on a stack of pillows. A plate of food is laid out before him.

I settle on some pillows near Sobek. A priest sets a plate before me. Other minions cover it with different delicacies. The scents are interesting but not enticing. I nibble at a few pieces in order to be polite.

Camilla is led in by a group of Sobek's priestesses. My heart stops. She looks stunning in a green sheath dress. Like me and Sobek, Camilla sits on a nest of pillows while her plate is loaded with food. Unlike me, she eats the meal with relish.

We spend time chatting about the food and fine weather. I try to raise the question of the egg, but Sobek is very specific that we shouldn't talk about anything related to Set until after the meal. I decide to respect his generosity by following his rules.

The moon is high in the night sky when Sobek turns his attention to our problems with Set.

"You wish to cast a spell and control chaos," announces Sobek.

"That's right," I say. "Isis gave us a map for a spell. We need a golden egg to serve as one ingredient."

"Ah." Sobek nods his great head. "And once you have these ingredients, you will return to the Red Pyramid and recast the spell to imprison Set."

Camilla nods. "Correct."

"This is a noble aim," says Sobek. "Yet, it remains a fool's errand."

"So we've been told," I counter. "Isis believes we should do nothing."

"And Thoth is setting up his own underground realm to outlive the destruction of Earth," adds Camilla. "What do you say?"

"You may consider my point of view as something between those two extremes. I don't think that chaos and destruction is unavoidable. Yet, I also do not support hiding away in your own realm, either. There are other things to try, though."

I give Sobek my most winning grin. "We've already settled on something to try. The spell. That's why we need an egg."

"Perhaps there is another option here," counters Sobek. "It's a chance to find something to save. Or to be specific, some*one* to keep alive forever."

His words echo through me in strange ways. I look over to Camilla. Moonlight casts her in a halo of blue. What if she could live through all eternity? Isn't a woman like her worth it?

Sobek tosses a handful of dates into his long maw. "I see you understand me, Xavier."

Camilla frowns. "I don't."

"What if I could keep you two here in my oasis forever? You'd be happy and safe." Here, Sobek looks straight at Camilla. "As well as perfectly healthy."

The world takes on a dream-like sheen. "You can really do that?"

"Each of us has our own gifts," says Sobek. "My magic concerns fertility and life. My oasis is more than a magical place hidden from humans. I don't need the tricks of Thoth. What I bring on the ground of my small home always thrives."

All of a sudden, I see me and Camilla spending an eternity here.

It's more than I ever imagined was possible. After all, there's no cure for khrysonia. Camilla is only returning to the future to face her own death.

Sobek rises. "These things are best seen to be understood."

Camilla stands as well. "You said you could help us. We need an egg."

"Follow me," says Sobek. "I will give you that ingredient… as well as a chance at a different life."

Sobek walks off. I step up to Camilla's side. "What do you think?"

"I think it's a lot of talk until we see ourselves a damned egg." She holds out her arm. Within seconds, her silver satchel materializes in her hand. Camilla zips the bag open and checks the map inside. "It still says Sobek is the one who can get us the egg."

All this while, Sobek has been striding across the courtyard. Now, Camilla and I follow him into another set of buildings. This time, the pool has a series of raised steps in the water that lead into a central house. Once we catch up with Sobek, he points to the edge of the pool.

"Wait here," Sobek commands. He crosses the stepping stones that lead over the pool itself. Although Sobek is a large figure, he easily marches into the little house. When Sobek comes out again, he carries a golden egg in his hands. "And here it is."

Sobek strides back across the stepping stones to join us at our side of the pool. Camilla holds out her hands. "Thank you."

Sobek keeps a firm grip on the egg. "Not yet. You need to meet my friend. She's the one who is offering this gift to you. If you decide to take it, then she is the one who deserves your thanks."

Sobek's words—*if you decide to take it*—rattle around my mind. What is Sobek planning, exactly?

Another long crocodile-type snout pops out from the dwelling in the center of the pool. A creature follows Sobek's path across the stepping stones. I've never seen anything like it.

Camilla gasps. "It's a dinosaur."

I scan the animal over and over. Camilla is right. Somehow, Sobek has kept one of the great lizards alive. None of these creatures should have survived Set's last purge of life in this world.

But Sobek saved this one. And that might open up a different future for both Camilla and me.

Sobek's Pet

30

XAVIER

The moment crystallizes in my mind. There's Sobek, holding the small golden egg that can help us cast the spell to stop Set. Beside him is Camilla, whose face is a mask of calm. I've no idea what she's thinking. And there's me. My heart thuds in my chest.

Camilla can be healed.

"As you can see," says Sobek. "I don't have enough power to keep an entire realm protected, but I do wield enough magic to protect the two of you."

"And you can heal Camilla?"

"Yes."

Camilla's eyes narrow. "How?"

"You'll become one of my daughters. Your appearance will change, but your memories will stay the same. As long as you and Xavier do not leave this oasis, you will never fall ill or die."

Camilla turns to me. "And what do you say?"

"I wouldn't care if your appearance changed. And I certainly don't mind staying in these buildings for all eternity. As long as I knew you'd be healthy and well, that's enough for me."

Camilla smiles, but there's no joy in her expression. "And what would happen when the rest of the world burns?"

In that instant, I know what she means. I'd been so excited by Sobek's offer, I hadn't thought through the full consequences. "We couldn't enjoy our eternity if it cost everyone else their mortal lives."

Camilla nods. "That's my Xavier."

"This is not a wise decision," says Sobek. "Still, I will respect what you have chosen." He extends his arms forward and offers the egg.

I take the object from his hands. "This is heavy."

"It's all gold and magic." Sobek sighs. "I would have enjoyed your company throughout eternity."

"It's not too late," I offer. "You can still join us at the Red Pyramid. Having you cast the spell with me and Camilla would only make things stronger."

"Here is where our paths diverge, I'm afraid." Sobek shakes his head. "What you wish to do is madness. Instead, I will keep looking out for someone else to add into my menagerie. Perhaps a human or two might be interested."

His words remind me of what Thoth said back at the crystal pyramid. Sobek wants to save a handful of chosen companions. Thoth wants to secure his own realm. Neither of them want to fight.

Sobek holds up his hand. Like the rest of his minions, Sobek's skin has the rough texture of a crocodile. "Before you leave, I would like you to answer one question, Xavier."

"You've been very kind," I state. "Whatever you ask, I'll do my best to answer."

"Why did Osiris choose to save you? For a long time, I thought it was because, like me, he likes to collect unusual creatures."

Again, I think back to that moment in my hut when golden magic appeared. That instance now seems so far away.

"I'll tell you what I've told everyone else who's asked me. I don't know."

"Ah, that's such as shame." Sobek bows. "Good night and better luck to you both." Sobek marches back into the dining room. His priests and priestesses follow.

I set the egg into my satchel and focus on Camilla. "That makes our second ingredient. All that remains is the mummy wrappings."

Camilla checks the map again. "I don't think you're going to like this."

And as it turns out, I don't.

Horus

31

XAVIER

Horus.

Why did it have to be Horus?

It's true that Horus is famous for his party games and magical awards. It wouldn't be unusual for him to give out mummy wrappings, a tooth, and a golden egg, all in one night.

Still, Horus is also a drunkard and a horse's ass. All of which is why I've been dreading this encounter ever since I left behind Kha and the Red Pyramid. It's true that Horus cast the spell to imprison Set, but Isis wasn't wrong about how she summed everything up. *Horus out-chaosed chaos.*

Camilla resets the map into her satchel. "Even I know where to find Horus. He runs a nightly celebration at the bottom of the Nile." She turns to me. There's no mistaking the ice in her stare. "You don't think you're my Xavier."

"I wish I were. Truly."

"Do you still think I'm Set's spy?"

"Set visited me in the Northlands. Almost every word you've spoken—or action you've taken—was predicted by the God of Chaos. I may not be your Xavier, but I know you now. You came here from another reality to save us. Thank you."

"That's something, I guess." Camilla lets out a long breath. "Let's grab that mummy wrapping and cast the spell."

We share a smile. I scoop Camilla into my arms and take to the air. The fastest path to the Nile takes us over the Palace of Akhet. Looking at my old home makes my throat tighten with sorrow.

Camilla leans her head against my shoulder. "You're thinking of him, aren't you? Osiris."

"What Isis said is true. Osiris believed he could fight Set and gain new power to control chaos."

Camilla rests her palm against my bare chest. "He *did* gain new power though, right?"

"He became the God of Duat, the underworld. And since Osiris had to reincarnate himself to come back to life, he gained power over that as well. But it wasn't enough magic to defeat Set."

"Have you seen him since the fight with Set?"

"Angels can't enter the underworld without a special key." I take in a deep breath. "And I've been ashamed to visit, Camilla. I should never have allowed my friend and brother to fight Set alone. Osiris saved my life by plucking me from that battlefield. He taught me magic, which is what's kept me alive all these years. I didn't protect him." I pull Camilla closer against me. "But for as long as you're here, I won't fail to keep you safe."

"Thank you." Camilla's voice carries an odd warble.

"Are you well?"

"Fine." *Which is a lie.* Camilla shivers in my arms, but not from cold. I scan her carefully. Her skin is far too pale to be healthy.

The landscape changes below us as we near the Nile. Once again, I see the dock where Camilla and I tied up her barque. The vessel still bobs in the water, just where we left it. We tied up the boat only a few days ago, but it feels as if a lifetime has passed since then.

I swoop down to land on the dock. Human voices echo through the night air. A steady stream of vessels float down the Nile. Like before, no humans can detect either the dock or anyone who stands upon it. In other words, this is the perfect spot to enter both the Nile and Horus' party.

I take extra care when setting Camilla on her feet. She steps to the edge of the dock and looks down into the dark water. "How do we get to the party?"

"Since it's nighttime, I can cast a spell to enter the celebration." I move to stand at Camilla's side. "Before I do so, how about something to eat or drink?"

"I just finished a feast at Sobek's oasis." She shoots me a sideways glance. "What's your worry?"

"You don't look well."

Camilla rubs her neck. "You're not wrong."

"Perhaps you should take your medicine before we enter the celebration."

Camilla shakes her head. "I just applied a patch a few hours ago. I'm not due for another full day." Even as she says those words, Camilla wobbles from foot to foot.

I hold out my hand. "You satchel, please."

Camilla nibbles her lower lip. "I won't have enough to last me through the rendezvous point."

I tilt my head. "And what happens if you arrive at the spot early?"

"Walker will pick me up if I get there before the rendezvous time. The only real problem is if I'm late."

"So, we apply the patch, hit the party, and then cast the spell at the Red Pyramid. This will be over quickly. You need to be healthy through it all… and then return to where you can take more medicine."

Camilla hugs her elbows. "Right."

The way she says that single word—*right*—makes me wonder if more medicine will make any difference. "How long do you have, Camilla?"

"More than enough to imprison Set again," she replies. Camilla lifts her arm. Her silver satchel materializes in her grip. She hands the bag over.

Having watched Camilla so many times, I know how to zip the container open. I pull out the red packet.

At the same time, Camilla rips off the most recent patch from her upper arm. The swirl mark is still there, only it's larger and darker than before. Worry twists inside me.

This isn't good.

I open the latest patch and set it on her palm. Camilla places the fabric on her upper arm and clutches at the spot. "Better."

Camilla shivers now, only it isn't from illness or the cold. Somehow, I know she's afraid. And I also know what to do. I step forward and envelop her in a hug. She leans into my shoulder.

"Too fast, too fast," she murmurs. "This isn't the first time I've placed on a patch early since arriving here."

"How many do you have left?"

"That's the last one."

"Would it help if I cast a healing spell?"

"Unfortunately, no" She looks up. "In my world, magic doesn't react well with technology."

I rub her back in slow circles. *My poor Camilla.*

"When I first met you, I was serving in Purgatory's Senate," she begins. "You were the diplomatic envoy from Heaven. I'd been preparing for your arrival. You barged in without an appointment. I accused you of using angelic influence to get your way with other diplomats."

"Angelic influence," I repeat. "That's an archangel power. Your Xav—" I stop myself before saying the words, *your Xavier*. "If anyone has that power, I'd imagine it would be tempting to use it, often."

Camilla loops her arms around my waist. "You tried it on me. I tossed you out of my office. You came back with ice cream, one cone for each of us. Have you heard of ice cream?"

"Aquila has told me."

"You wouldn't leave until we'd stopped for a bit and finished our cones." She looks up at me. "You're my Xavier. When we see each other again, it will be the first time for me, do you understand?"

"I do." *Even though it won't be me.*

"Don't forget those ice cream cones."

My heart cracks. Tears pool in my eyes. "Camilla, I don't know what to say."

She goes on tiptoe and kisses my cheek. "Let's do this."

I search my mind for any solution that might heal Camilla. There's nothing. The most I can do is honor the reason she came here.

We must get the ingredient, cast the spell, and stop Set.

32

XAVIER

After pulling a fresh spell packet from my satchel, I move to stand by the edge of the dock. While crushing the ingredients in my fist, I whisper the incantation.

Open I go
Travel and flow

Energy and magic move down my arm. The packet erupts with light. I twist my wrist so the brightness shines onto the darkened waters of the Nile. Liquid churns under the magic. A rectangular-shaped hole appears in the surface. Watery steps descend. More water rises until it congeals into a liquid staircase that ends right at the dock's edge.

I offer Camilla my arm. She still wears the green shift dress from Sobek's dinner. It clings to her curves in all the right ways. *So beautiful.*

Camilla gently rests her hand on my forearm. She eyes the liquid staircase. "I haven't walked down one of these in a while."

"They have magic underwater parties in the future?"

Camilla chuckles. "Often."

I picture Camilla and her Xavier walking into other celebrations like this one. Only at these events, Camilla really belongs to her husband and mate. That isn't me. I push the thought aside and focus on Set.

Together, Camilla and I descend. The stairs may appear to be liquid, but they're actually solid to the touch. It's the walls and ceiling that are more gelatinous. We process downward until the dark waters envelop us.

Halfway there.

Camilla and I continue our descent until the dark waters below us glow with far-off light. That's Horus' garden, the place where he holds his evening celebrations. The staircase ends. We step into the party itself.

Palm trees encircle an open courtyard. The floor is the same liquid as the stairs—gelatinous to the eye but solid underfoot. All around us, the walls and ceiling are sheets of dark liquid that slowly undulate with the rhythms of the Nile.

Different games are set up around the periphery of the space. There are tables with board games like senet or jackals and hounds. Partygoers meander around the scene. The ladies wear white linen sheath dresses. The men don matching white kilts.

"You weren't kidding about the games," whispers Camilla. "All this place is missing is face painting and pin the tail on the demon."

"Like Isis said, Horus isn't the most mature deity around."

"So, Horus is the *forever a boy* type?"

"Somewhat. He's also the kind who likes to be surrounded by admirers."

"How so?"

"Years ago, Isis and Osiris would host parties here. Back then, the place would be filled with all sorts of guests. There would be hippo-faced followers from Taweret… clay men and women born of the potter's wheel of Khnum… and even the feline-humans who follow the cat goddess, Bast."

"Everyone here tonight has little feathers instead of skin."

"They're all followers of Horus."

"Attendance is mandatory, then."

"You guessed it."

Camilla sniffs. "Nothing is less festive than being forced into a party. Where do you think Horus is hiding the mummy wrappings?"

"Horus calls out regular competitions throughout the night." I gesture around the periphery of the room. "Winners may request a prize from anything that hangs from a palm frond."

Camilla points to a shiny item which hangs from a nearby tree. "Is that a golden arm cuff?"

"Yes." I scan the other items suspended nearby. "That must be the jewelry section. The next set of trees have prizes that augment beauty, like jugs of oil and vials of perfume."

Camilla gives my arm a squeeze. "And the last group of trees have stuff to prepare for the afterlife. There are canopic jars, boxes of incense, and—*there!*—a ball of linen wrappings. Do you see it?"

"I do." And I grin rather widely as I say those two words.

"What's the fastest way to get them and go?"

"This is Horus' party. If we want any of the prizes, we must win one of Horus' games. He gets ever so touchy about anyone stealing his prizes."

"Like a true game show host."

I frown. "I'm afraid I don't know that reference from the future."

"It means Horus is the type that's far easier to placate than fight."

"Exactly."

Speaking of Horus, he steps out from behind a group of partygoers. Horus stands seven feet tall and wears the golden kilt and adornments of a pharaoh. While he has a human body, Horus' head is that of a hawk. He points his clawed hand in our direction.

"Newcomers!" cries Horus. "Woooooo!"

"Is he—" begins Camilla.

"Drunk?" I ask. "Yes. And it isn't easy for a deity to become drunk. Clearly, Horus has accomplished that state and then some."

"Come over and hear my story," cries Horus. "I'm about to tell the great saga of how I imprisoned my father's murderer, Set."

I cup my hand by my mouth. "We'll be right there!" I turn to Camilla. "Ready?"

She opens her mouth to speak, then pauses. While hissing in a breath, Camilla grabs her shoulder. Worry twists inside me. Camilla is gripping the spot where she last placed her medicine patch.

I move to stand before her and cup her face in my hands. "I promised myself to keep you safe. If this is too much, I can face Horus alone."

Camilla lets out a long breath. "No, we'll do this together."

Across the garden, Horus raises his arms. "Come over, my friends! Do not leave your host waiting!"

Camilla smirks. "Now, are *you* ready?"

"So ready," I reply.

We walk toward Horus together.

Horus

33

XAVIER

Horus keeps waving us over. "Come closer, it's time to pick a new game."

Camilla and I join the group of minions who surround him. All seem to hang on his every word.

Up close, Horus appears even drunker than I thought. Here I am, his father's best friend, and Horus doesn't even notice.

"I have an idea." As Horus speaks, he visibly wobbles from foot to foot. "How about we have another swimming competition?" While the staircase was solid, most of the chamber here is more gelatinous. Horus marches over to a nearby wall and sets his arm directly into the water wall. "Feels warm enough to me."

His minions beam with joy.

"Yes, a swim," says one.

"Love this idea," adds a second.

"I'll go first," cries a third.

Horus steps away. "On second thought, I'm tired of coming up with all the ideas for games. Why don't you all suggest some?"

A long pause follows while no one wants to be the first with an idea.

"Let's do something with music," says Camilla.

"Yes, summon the players," calls someone else.

Everyone joins in some version of "time for a dance."

"Ah! A dance contest." Horus' bird-eyes loll in his head before his gaze locks on me. "What do you think?"

I shrug. "That's fine."

"Hey!" Horus points his claw finger at me. "You're my father's best friend. I remember you."

"I recall you as well."

"You're the one who cares about those pathetic humans," says Horus.

I force my face into my best and most pleasant mask. "You protected humanity when you imprisoned Set."

"And now you cavort with one of Set's minions." Horus rounds on Camilla. "Are you excited your master will soon be free?"

"I'm a daughter of Purgatory," says Camilla calmly. Her tail arches over her shoulder to wave at Horus. "Which means I'm mostly human."

Horus bobs his head back and forth. It's an especially bird-like move. "How will that tail save you when Set eventually breaks free? He's coming for you all."

I set my hand on Camilla's hip. "She's not alone. Because if Set destroys life on Earth, you'll be dead, too."

A long moment passes while Horus sizes me up. It's as if he's seeing me for the first time. "I locked Set up. He's not coming back."

At these words, the ground rumbles. Water streams down the walls to pool on the floor. Wisps of red smoke rise up.

"We need your help," I state. "Set is breaking free."

"Ask my father. He always did as you wished."

"You can visit him easily. I cannot."

Horus steps closer. "Why are you here?"

"Xavier and I are recasting the spells on the Red Pyramid," says Camilla. "We need the linen mummy wrappings on that palm." She points to the tree in question.

"I'll give them to you as a gift. But nothing is free. I want something in exchange."

"And what is that?" asks Camilla.

"An honest answer." Horus pins me with a desperate look. "From you."

"I know what you'll ask, because everyone poses the same question. Why did Osiris choose to save me from the battlefield?"

Horus nods.

"You'll get the same answer. I honestly don't know."

Horus lets out a piercing screech. "It's not fair! Father likes you better than me and you don't even know why!"

I scan the distance between our spot and the palm tree. So does Camilla.

"Are you thinking what I'm thinking?" she asks.

I nod. "You grab the linen wrappings. I'll do the rest."

"Right."

I scoop Camilla into my arms, extend my wings and make for the tree. Horus bares his claws and races after us. He also tries to unfurl his wings in order to fly. Fortunately, Horus is too drunk to actually get airborne.

I fly in a straight line for the palm. Camilla grabs the mummy wrappings as we race by.

"Take a deep breath and hold tight," I call.

Camilla curls up against me as I fly right into the liquid wall and beyond. My wings aren't as efficient in water as they are in the air, but it's still enough.

Once we break free from the Nile, I keep momentum and return to the skies. As we fly away, Horus surfaces in the waters below us.

"Coward!" Horus calls. "Weakling! Come back here and fight!"

He's not wrong. After all, I am the least powerful warrior in Heaven. But I'm also the one with Camilla in my arms and a spell to imprison Set.

Things are looking up.

Red Pyramid

34

XAVIER

It's still dark when Camilla and I reach the Red Pyramid. We touch down at the top of the staircase. The front door is open.

"This is wrong," I state. "This door shouldn't be open until the artisans arrive at dawn."

"Should we wait for them artisans, or at least get Kha?"

I remember the time I tried to help Kha cast the imprisonment spell. "There's no need to fetch him. For this spell, the power is all in the ingredients."

"This doesn't feel right."

"Agreed. We should go slowly."

For the first time, I offer Camilla my hand. She laces her fingers with mine. Together, we step into the Great Temple Chamber. The room is empty. A stale scent hangs in the air. It takes a moment to adjust to the dim light.

That's when I see them.

Dead bodies lie on the floor. Tools are strewn all around. All the breath leaves my lungs. "There are four levels below this chamber. We need to reach the lowest one and cast the spell, fast." I speed to the opened door at the far end of the chamber. "There isn't room for me to fly."

"Let's run."

Camilla and I race through the passage to the chamber below. Before, that room has been filled with trees and the wooden hawk. Now the trees are overturned. More bodies lie on the floor. The wooden bird lies smashed into kindling.

We rush to the next chamber. Again the room is ruined. The wooden hound has been torn apart. Worry careens through my system. This can't be happening.

The final chamber is another disaster. All the sarcophagi lie shattered on the floor, along with newly dead bodies.

We race to the last level. Here, the pit still sits in the center of the room. Kha lies nearby on the floor. We rush to his side. Camilla sets her hand on his neck.

"He's dead," she says in a low voice.

I check his hands. "He's not carrying any ingredients. He must have just cast the spell."

Camilla looks into the pit. "It's dark. What does that mean?"

"Set is imprisoned down there," I explain. "If the pit is dark, then the spell is holding."

"So who killed everyone in the pyramid?"

"I don't know. When Set visited my hut in the Northlands, he pretended to threaten my friend, Mortimer. But it was all an illusion. Set was still imprisoned here."

Camilla hugs her elbows. "Do you think this is an illusion, too?"

"Hard to tell. I can cast a spell to be certain... but *after* we finish resealing this prison."

"I don't cast spells," says Camilla. "How can I help?"

"Hand me the ingredients when I need them. As I said before, they do all the work. First the egg. Second, the tooth. Third, the wrappings."

I move to stand by the edge of the pit. Camilla gathers the ingredients from our respective satchels. Once we're ready, I speak the incantation.

We seal this room with potential.

As I speak the word *wisdom,* Camilla hands me the egg. I drop it into the pit. Tendrils of red mist rise from the chamber below.

Camilla frowns. "Is that right?"

I nod. "This is what happened before." I continue with the spell.

We lock this room with strength.

Camilla hands me the golden fang. I drop it into the darkness. More lines of red mist rise up. I keep going.

Through the power of lives past, we close this chamber for the future.

I take the mummy wrappings from Camilla and drop them into the pit as well. All the cords of red mist retract into the dark. A crimson light flares brightly in the pit. It then dims to perfect blackness.

Moments pass. Neither of us feel like we should breathe, let alone move. Still, the pit remains dark. Set is imprisoned. It's over.

"That went well," I state.

"Sometimes, things work out."

"We did it."

Camilla smiles. "Together."

Both of us melt into a hug. I love the feeling of having her in my arms. Still, I force myself to step away. There's another spell to cast here. After grabbing a fresh packet of ingredients, I kneel beside Kha and cast the spell to break illusions.

Truth and dawn
Lies be gone

Energy and magic surge up my arms. White light erupts from the ingredients I've crushed in my fist. Pale beams shine out onto Kha. His body flickers in and out of existence.

Then, it vanishes.

A chill crawls up my back. "This is an illusion," I state. "Kha isn't really here."

"What about everything else?" asks Camilla.

"Probably an illusion as well."

A low chuckle echoes through the room. Red light shines up from the pit, casting the room in shifting shadows. I lock gazes with Camilla before looking into the pit.

It's no longer dark. Red light shines within. And inside that brightness, I see a face.

It's Set.

"I'm free," he intones. "And I have been for a very long time."

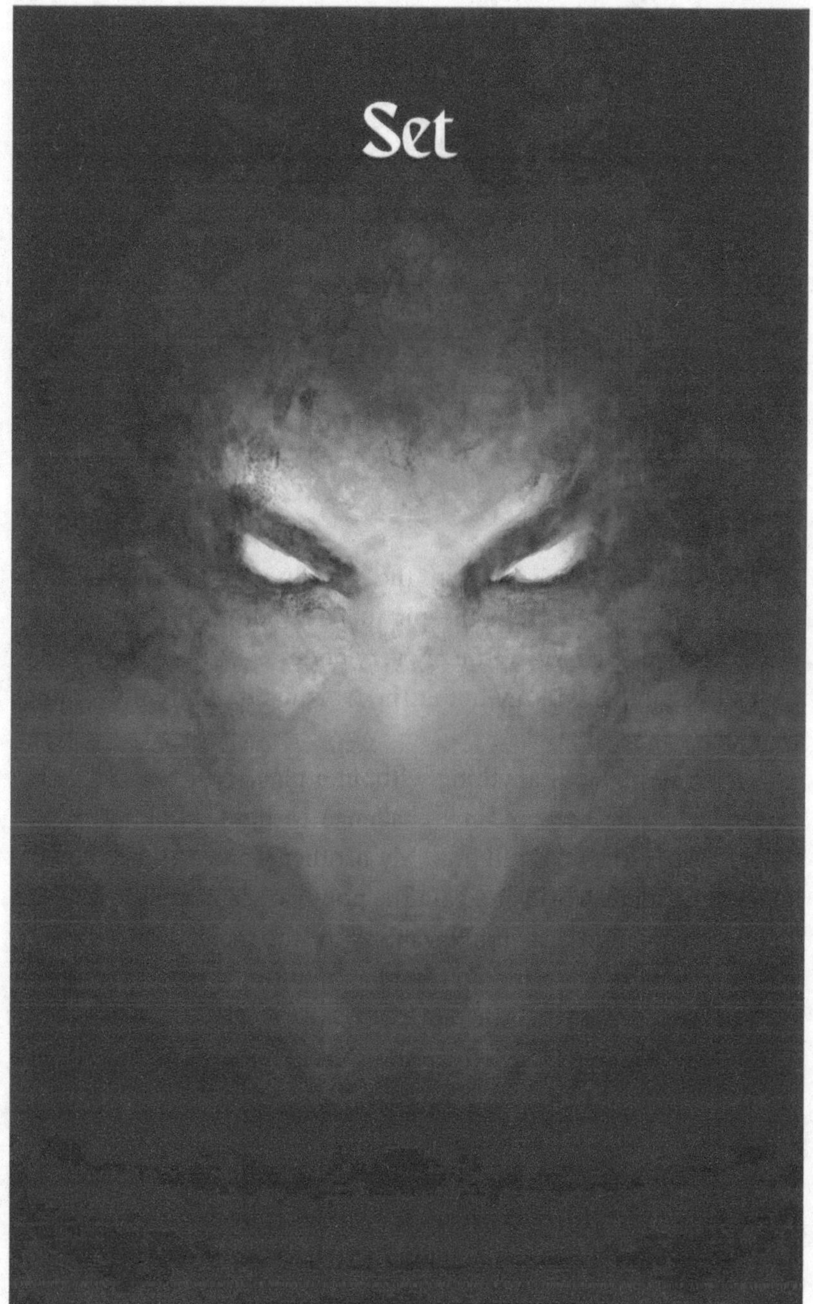
Set

35

XAVIER

Set slowly rises from the opening in the floor. Light flickers up from the pit to flash across his dark robes. Waves of chaotic energy rattle my very bones.

It's like I'm back in my hut at the Northlands. Only now, things are much worse.

"Osiris never does anything without a plan," says Set. "He had a scheme when he accepted my challenge to fight. Looking back, I believe Osiris knew I'd kill him. My brother wanted to become the ruler of the underworld and gain the power of reincarnation. Osiris thought that would give him the ability to stop me. It didn't work."

"I'll stay here," I whisper to Camilla. "You run."

"I'm not leaving you," she replies.

"So, my thoughts turned to you, Xavier. Osiris wouldn't have saved you unless there was a purpose. Perhaps you're the key to my brother's plans. So, I allowed myself to be tossed into this prison. Then I schemed and waited. You ran away. It took years to find you. Then, even more time passed while I put you through all my tests."

"That's what this was all about," I state. "Isis, Sobek, Thoth and Horus… those were all tests. You wanted to see if I'd expose anything about Osiris' plans."

"Yes," confirms Set. "And you didn't reveal anything of value. Which means all of this was a waste. There's actually no way you can stop me from ending this world. And to punish you for consuming my thoughts, I'll begin my destruction of all life by ruining yours." Set snaps his fingers. Camilla gasps.

Looking over, I see what has upset her. Set has burned the medicine patch off Camilla's arm. She gasps and leans over. I scoop her into my arms.

Camilla turns pale. She shivers uncontrollably. Her skin breaks out in a thin sheen of sweat.

At the same time, magic and smoke erupts from the pit. Ghostly faces appear in the swirling red cloud. All of them scream without making a sound. The shining red haze presses in and around the room. The very stones around us pull apart.

The Red Pyramid explodes. Brick, plaster and bodies fly off in every direction. I'm barely aware that I now sit beside an open pit in an otherwise-deserted landscape. Camilla's dying body is cradled in my arms. In this moment, nothing else seems to matter.

A column of Set's red magic blasts up into the clouds before rolling back down to the ground. A miasma of chaos then rolls out over the countryside, leaving a never-ending swath of red smoke and fire in its wake. Screams rend through the air. People are being exterminated, just as Set promised.

This is really happening. Set is wiping out the world.

Somehow, I can't process anything outside of a single fact.

Camilla is dying.

And that changes everything.

Miasma of Chaos

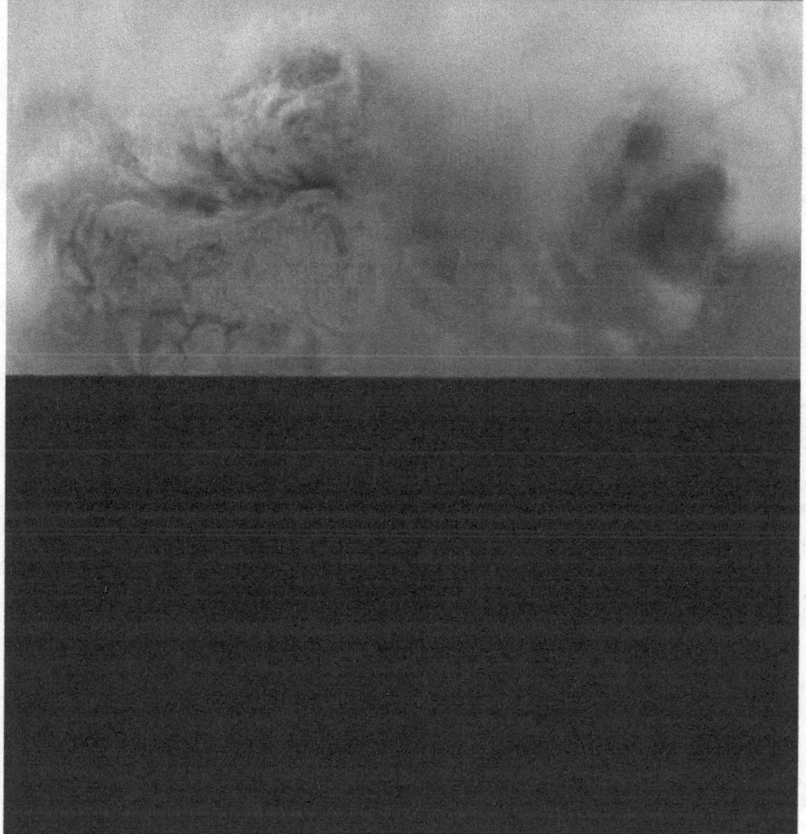

36

XAVIER

Sitting down, I extend my wings to create a cocoon around me and Camilla. I cradle her body in my left arm and on my lap. A line of blood runs in a thin rivulet from her ear. With my right hand, I brush my fingers along her jawline.

"What's happening?" she asks.

"I'm with you. You're safe."

She smiles, only there's no joy in the expression. "When this is done, take me to the Dashur Mines. If Walker is still alive, he'll bring me back. I want to be buried with my family."

My eyes burn with held-in tears. "What kind of family do you have?"

"We have children, Xavier. And grandchildren, too." Her breathing turns ragged. "Some of them are dragons."

Somehow, I'm able to choke out a few words. "That's beautiful."

I rock her gently from side to side. Camilla closes her eyes and drifts into an uneasy sleep. Meanwhile, my soul burns with grief and rage. *Nothing is worse than this.* How did *her* Xavier ever exist while knowing he would lose her… and that *he* was the one who caused her death.

Every part of my body seems to freeze. For the first time, I understand this Xavier. How he feels. Who he loves. What he'd do to keep Camilla.

Connections happen.

Memories align.

Powers awaken.

For the first time since the Northlands, a unique kind of magic truly stirs within me. New power whirls through my veins. My hands glow with golden light.

Images appear in my mind. They are not from my own consciousness. All of a sudden, I remember meeting Camilla for the first time. The recollection is so clear and real. We're in Purgatory's Senate, sharing rocky road ice cream cones. I'm in awe of how quickly I feel a connection to this woman. There's longing. Trust. Attraction. It's all present back then, just as it was when I first saw Camilla in my dreams.

Another revelation appears. *I don't just understand this Xavier. I am this Xavier.* These memories are from my own future.

More instances appear. I recall when the first wispy marks materialized on Camilla's arm. *Khrysonia.* I didn't believe it was true. After all, Camilla and I had been together for so long. In all those years, there was never been any sign of this dreaded disease. Now, khrysonia was killing Camilla. We tried every type of medicine and spell. Nothing helped.

Still, I wouldn't accept that she would not only die, she'd be erased from any afterlife.

At the same time, chaos magic entered our existence. The very fabric of reality began to fray. The world focused on saving itself. For my part, I couldn't see past Camilla's death sentence. I kept searching every archive and spell for a cure. At the same time, my noble Camilla focused on saving the world from chaos.

Eventually, I came across the story of Set and Osiris. An idea formed. Perhaps Osiris' reincarnation magic could help.

Once the idea appeared, I couldn't let it go. I needed to see Osiris and ask for his help. That wouldn't be easy. So, I broke into the Palace of Akhet and stole a golden ankh, which is the only key that I could use to open the doors to Duat, the underworld ruled by Osiris.

I broke into Osiris' throne room and demanded that he heal my wife. The God of the Underworld listened to my pleas before declaring, "there is no way to cure khrysonia."

More magic churns through me. Soon, my entire body glows with golden light. Camilla still rests. In my mind, I'm back in the Duat throne room, re-experiencing my future conversation with Osiris.

"Please, there must be a spell."

Osiris frowns. "If such magic existed, it would be enough to undo chaos itself."

"In that case, I'll find the magic to end chaos."

Osiris considers my words. "Set cannot be killed, but perhaps he can be contained. I've always thought it was possible. That's why I became ruler of the underworld—I thought I'd gain the power to contain Set. It wasn't enough, though. But, perhaps if my new abilities combine with your archangel magic, something could be done."

"What are you thinking about? I'll try anything."

"You'd need to learn magic for years."

"I'll start now."

"Impossible. You would need to have begun the training thousands of years ago. The secret to spell casting is repetition. Eons of repetition."

"Then reincarnate me. Send me back to the beginning of my life, only lock away my archangel power. I'll find you and learn magic."

Osiris drums his fingers on the arm of his golden throne. "If I lock away your power, you won't remember who you are. I'll need to find you and train you as a regular, low-level angel... which is possible. Even then, it's unlikely that you'll remember who you are and regain your power."

"Try me."

"And if you should imprison Set, there's no guarantee you'll save Camilla."

"I disagree. Give me another chance, and I'll stay away from Camilla unless I find a cure for khrysonia. I'll have thousands of years to search for one."

"It's an interesting bargain. But remember this: Set is clever. He knows I wish to imprison him. He may suspect our arrangement. That won't go well for you."

"Give me a chance. I will do this."

"Yes, I think if anyone can, it would be you."

It feels as if ages go by while I regain my memories. In reality, only a few seconds pass.

Camilla flutters her eyes open. "You're golden."

"I remember everything now. I made a deal with Osiris to be reincarnated on the same timeline. Only, I came back with my memories erased and my archangel powers suppressed."

"Why?"

"You, Camilla. I must discover a cure for khrysonia. Now, I have thousands of years to find one. And since one must always make a bargain with the gods, I promised to do something for Osiris in return. Imprison Set."

"You will." Camilla brushes her fingertips across my lips. "Say it."

"I'm your Xavier."

"Show me."

I keep my wings enclosed around Camilla and me. At the same time, I tap into my golden magic within. More energy moves through my limbs. I grow taller. My muscles thicken. My wings turn golden as well. I become the archangel Xavier.

I lean in and kiss her gently. "My Camilla."

"My Xavier." She sighs. "Now, I hauled my ass through time to stop Set. I'll rest right here while you do your thing." She adds four words that fire my soul.

"Go kick his ass."

Xavier

37

XAVIER

I force my wings to unfold from around Camilla. With gentle movements, I shift her from my lap to rest on the rocky ground. As I rise to my full height, my old memories of battle tactics swim through my thoughts. I recall pulling on my angelic energy to strike or outmaneuver an enemy.

Now, I focus that same power in a new direction: magic.

My experiences and power weave together. I don't need ingredients for a spell. Those things are for casters without enough natural magic. I now have plenty.

Beyond our little stretch of rocky ground, the rest of the world burns. Chaos smoke rises in every direction. Screams echo across a red landscape. To repair this horror, I need my magic.

So, I gaze upon Camilla. She lies on one side, reclining in a way that reminds me of a Greek goddess statue. She cradles her arm beneath her head, allowing her red hair to spread around her like a halo. All the love and faith in the world shines in her brown eyes. She knows I can do this.

I feel a thousand feet tall.

My love for her taps into my deepest power. Our gazes lock. I think about all the couples across this earth who adore each other as much as me and my bride. I want them to have another chance, too. I call an incantation of summoning.

I call upon the skies, bring forth my enemy
I order the earth, deliver my foe

Lightning strikes the ground nearby. Raising my arms, I direct another cry to the heavens.

Set! I summon thee!

Golden light shines from my palms, creating a beacon into the red sky. Power moves from my deepest self and into the clouds. I sense more than see Set appear before me. I lower my hands. The beams of golden light die out for now.

Sure enough, Set stands before me. "You do have a little bit of magic after all. I knew Osiris was scheming something. Do you wish to do battle?"

"Yes."

"How very like Osiris you are." Set lifts his arm. A long sword materializes in his hand. The blade drips with blood. "I'll enjoy this fight."

"As am I." *Only I won't fight in the way you expect.*

I summon more inner magic. Golden light collects on my palms. I press more power through my arms. A column of golden brightness erupts from my hands. Before, I sent the power into the sky. Now, I focus it in a new direction.

Set's prison.

While my light and energy fly into the darkened pit, I call out Kha's spell.

We seal this room with potential.

Set stalks toward me while raising his blade. The God of Chaos tries to strike my heart, yet his weapon crumples against me. I keep pouring light and energy into the dark pit.

We lock this room with strength.

Set tosses the sword aside and stalks away. He doesn't get far before tendrils of golden light erupt from the pit. These new cords wrap about Set's ankles, dragging him back into his new prison.

More golden light rolls off my hands and into the pit. At the same time, Set gets dragged back into his underground dungeon. The God of Chaos claws at the earth, but it's no use. My magic drags him back into the onyx prison as I finish the incantation.

Through the power of lives past, we close this chamber for the future.

A final blast of golden power erupts from the pit before it all darkens once more. This time, the pit isn't dark and open. It's sealed with sheet of gold.

Kneeling down, I draw Camilla into my arms again. She tries to force a smile, but only the corner of her mouth tips up. "You locked him up."

I kiss her forehead. "I had lots of help."

Extending my wings, I take the skies once more. This time, I follow the quickest route to the Dashur Mines. Below me, the red miasma dissipates from the earth. Golden light rolls across the countryside. *My magic.* Everywhere my brightness touches, the world heals. Houses reform. Bodies that had been unmoving now come back to life. Even the many bricks of the Red Pyramid fly back into their familiar shape.

The sky lightens with the first signs of dawn as I fly over the lip to the Dashur Mines. I soar in slow circles to the valley's lowest point. From there, I wait for Walker to transport Camilla to her future reality.

It doesn't take long.

Xavier & Camilla

38

XAVIER

An orange sphere appears in the sky. Camilla lies curled in my arms. Inch by inch, she raises her gaze to scan the clouds.

"My transport is almost here." Camilla's gaze meets mine. And the strongest woman in the world proves her inner steel by admitting her greatest fear. "I don't want to go."

She's talking about more than the machine that will take her away from me. Camilla doesn't want to die.

"You aren't going anywhere," I state. "I will discover a cure for khrysonia. I have thousands of years to do it."

"No, Xavier." Camilla's voice turns faint and shaky. "Too long."

I know what she means. Camilla thinks that thousands of years are too long for me to be alone.

"Mark my words. I will wait for you. I will heal you. Nothing else matters."

The silver spiral lowers from the clouds. Orange lights blink along the interior. A low hum sounds as the tracking beacon locks in on Camilla. She slowly rises from my arms and enters the coil's center. The silver machine reacts into the sky until it resembles a far-off sphere once more.

The orange light blinks out of existence in this reality.

Camilla is gone.

"It will be thousands of years before I see you again," I whisper to the sky. "But, oh, you're worth every moment."

—The End—

Xavier and Camilla return in ARCHNEMESIS

ALSO BY CHRISTINA BAUER

ARCHNEMESIS

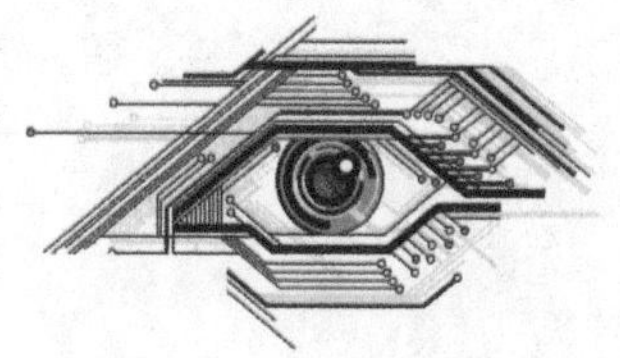

Xavier and Camilla return in ARCHNEMESIS…

EVIL QUEENS AND GOBLIN KINGS

BOOK 1, WITCHES OF THE MAGICORUM

ANGELBOUND

Check out ANGELBOUND, the kick-ass paranormal romance that started it all!

PIXIELAND DIARIES

PIXIELAND DIARIES tells the story of sassy pixie Calla and 'her' elf prince, Dare.

DIMENSION DRIFT

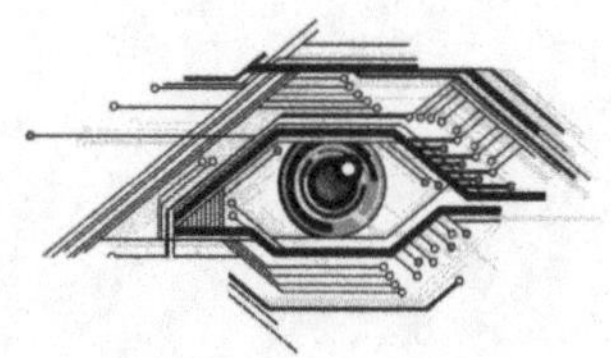

A kick-ass heroine + a swoon-worthy prince + an all-girl heist = SCYTHE!!!

BEHOLDER

Medieval mages ... Slow-burn love ... And heart-pounding action! Check out the BEHOLDER series!

APPENDIX

IF YOU ENJOYED THIS BOOK...

...Please consider leaving a review, even if it's just a line or two. Every bit truly helps, especially for those of us who don't *write by the numbers,* if you know what I mean.

Plus I have it on good authority that every time you review an indie author, somewhere an angel gets a mocha latte. For reals.

And angels need their caffeine, too.

ACKNOWLEDGMENTS

If you're reading my freaking acknowledgements, chances are, I should thank you for something. So, for the record: you are awesome, dear reader. Thank you.

That said, huge and heartfelt appreciation must go out to my husband and son for their rock-solid support. Being an author means a lot of early mornings, late nights, long weekends, and never-ending patience. You two are the best guys in the universe, period.

After that, I must thank the extensive network of reviewers, friends and colleagues who helped me build my writing chops in general. A especially loud shout out goes to my bestie, the lovely and talented Kim Stern (who also happens to be the original inspiration for Cissy from Angelbound).

Finally, deep affection goes out to my late, much loved, and dearly missed Aunt Sandy and Uncle Henry. You saw the writer in me, always. Thank you, first and last.

ABOUT CHRISTINA BAUER

Christina Bauer thinks that fantasy books are like bacon: they just make life better. All of which is why she writes romance novels that feature demons, dragons, wizards, witches, elves, elementals, and a bunch of random stuff that she brainstorms while riding the Boston T. Oh, and she includes lots of humor and kick-ass chicks, too. Christina lives in Newton, MA with her husband, son, and semi-insane golden retriever, Ruby.

Stalk Christina on Social Media

Blog:
http://monsterhousebooks.com/blog/category/christina

Facebook:
https://www.facebook.com/authorBauer/

Instagram:
https://www.instagram.com/christina_cb_bauer/

Twitter:
@CB_Bauer

VLOG:
https://tinyurl.com/Vlogbauer

Web site:
www.bauersbooks.com

SUBSCRIBE

Get a FREE copy of Christina Bauer's novella, BEVERLY HILLS VAMPIRE, when you sign up for her personal newsletter:

https://tinyurl.com/bauersbooks

Not available in stores

BEVERLY HILLS VAMPIRE

A NOVELLA BY CHRISTINA BAUER

BONUS IMAGES

Dear Reader,

Whenever I write a book, there is always a ton of world building that ends up on the 'virtual cutting-room floor' of my imagination. In this section, I'll give a quick tour of the edits that hurt the most in ARCHENEMY.

Originally, Xavier started off fighting gladiator-style in the real Roman Coliseum.... because what's a story in ancient times without gladiators? Also, these battles could be a nice parallel to what happens in the Angelbound Origins series.

Sadly, that grew into a gladiator book which battled hard with my ancient Egypt story. Basically, adding in all that gladiator stuff kept me from digging deeper into other world-building. In the end, I had to cut the storyline entirely. Instead, I started off with ancient England. This way, it gives a grounding of Xavier's regular life before moving on to his hero's journey into Egypt.

Nixing the gladiator stuff also gave me more room to build in the great myths of ancient Egypt, such as Isis, Osiris, Set and Horus. What's in the book is fairly close to the original with one big exception: Horus was not a douchebag.

With all that lead-up, here's an image of gladiator Xavier!

Xavier

ABOUT AURELIAN

Originally, this book carried a whole storyline about how the archangel Aurelian falls in love with a human woman named Merit. Aurelian's power focuses on righteous anger and chastity—the Heavenly opposites to the mortal sins of lust and wrath.

Aurelian's tale would highlight the consequences of an archangel experiencing true love with a human. But the stuff about Aurelian and Merit started stealing valuable spotlight from Xavier and Camilla. By changing the timeline so Camilla returns to ancient Egypt *after* she's showing signs of the disease called khrysonia, I could make the same point without diluting the main love story.

Here's a pic of Aurelian. I'm sure you can understand how miserable I was to delete him!

Aurelian

ABOUT MERIT

And here's Aurelian's love interest, Merit. Since Aurelian's magic is off the charts, his love for Merit causes her to contract khrysonia, a deadly disease that only affects true love partners that are archangel and human. The picture on the next page shows Merit with a khrysonia mark on her shoulder.

It's a cool photo, but I ended up being able to cover the same thing with Camilla without adding in the extra storyline.

Farewell, Merit!

Merit

ABOUT BORIS

Early on, I wanted to add stuff about aliens helping to create ancient Egypt… and then returning later on in order to help Set to destroy the planet. It's an interesting idea, only it confused the idea of Set as the main antagonist. The aliens simply had to go.

The character of Boris got lost along the way. He's a good alien who is trying to save Earth. The image on the next page shows Boris fiddling with the technology needed to defeat Senenmut, the evil alien leader of the story (more on Senenmut later). Boris was funny as Hell. Sadly, he was also a huge distraction.

Goodbye, friend!

Boris

ABOUT SENENMUT

Back to Senenmut, aka the antagonist of my lost storyline. Damn, did I ever love this guy. I even tinkered with adding in alternating chapters between Xavier and Camilla. That way, Camilla could fight evil future aliens while Xavier focused on Set in the past.

Senenmut was cool. Senenmut was badass. Ultimately, Senenmut was too much for this book. I needed to give Isis, Osiris and company more time to develop.

Ultimately, the Senenmut situation helped me realize something. Stories of ancient Egypt often focus on mummies or aliens instead of actual myths. The latest scholarship shows that what we call Greco-Roman myth is actually Greco-Roman-Egyptian. Isis went on the original Odyssey. Images of Isis with wings predate anything called an angel. And it was the Egyptian sun god Ra—not Apollo—who was first reported as steering a vehicle which brings up the dawn.

I love stories that explore mythic themes of life, love, death and power. The Greco-Roman-Egyptian canon is filled with great tales that I hope will inspire me for years to come.

And I hope you enjoy this image of Senenmut!
Christina Bauer

Senenmut

www.ingramcontent.com/pod-product-compliance
Lightning Source LLC
Chambersburg PA
CBHW010358310726
48979CB00006B/1081

* 9 7 8 1 9 5 6 1 1 4 5 2 2 *